Robert's Short Stories

BOOK III

ROBERT PORTER

authorHOUSE

AuthorHouse™
1663 Liberty Drive
Bloomington, IN 47403
www.authorhouse.com
Phone: 833-262-8899

Published by AuthorHouse 03/04/2021

ISBN: 978-1-6655-1907-6 (sc)
ISBN: 978-1-6655-1906-9 (e)

Print information available on the last page.

Contents

Nielson Morgan

NIELSON PUT ON A PAIR of blue denim jeans. The weather out was a little damp.

He expected that it might be damp, from the high grass his backyard had grown out, he had just returned home from a volunteer army camp out in the Rockies.

Nielson put on some thick black boots and thick army socks.

Walking out to the grass mowers shack; Nielson took out Morgan David Mower. A sharp w/ blacked mower. He also took out some shears and a couple rakes.

Pat Grandger a step son of Nielsons would join him later. The backyard lead to a garden of scquach it had just turned yellow from the hot scorching sun above their pine and apple tree.

Pat Grander used to cycle to cut off the tops of the grass once he did then Nielson ran the mower over the taps of the grass mowing it down to ¾ of an inch high. Both grabbed rakes and raked up the leaves that had fallen into a pile. Pat put them into bag, then dumped then into the dumpster across the parking lot. Tired from all the raking up of leaves.

Nielson went shopping for a leaf blower. He looked at all brands the store had in stock. Hoover; Sears; after checking the guarantees and expected life he went with an Electro Lucks it had the largest collection bag. He liked the reversing chair and the height it would go. Also it was a high powered vacuums. Nielson also liked the colors of choice; Red, red green; green blue; blue white yellow.

He also liked the wide 648 tires on the back and the 625 on the front.

Kind of reminded him of the 1951 Camero he built when he raced on a dirt track. It had 3 inch 9 pikes of hard rubber that grabbed the road. Morgan had it delivered to his back yard where he would be use it.

Eddie the delivery man put the keys in the mail box. He left a note enjoy your new toy Nielson laughed. He stood in front of it and enjoyed the way it looked setting on a dirt mound of high leafs.

Nielson could not wait any longer.

Nielson turned towards his back door; lifted his right front leg; tightened his left leg then with all his might shoved off rotating left; right; left; right only 8 times a piece before stepping on the starter of the snow blower instantly it sucked up a 2 inch pile of leaves.

Nielson pushed forward; as he did so the leaves were sucked up into the blower forward then in reverse, forward again until all the leaves had been sucked up into the bag fastened on the right side with 12 snap on pens going from left side to right side.

Nielson unsnapped the full bag of leaves, turned around the blower refastened the bag full of leaves then hit the up button.

Raising slowly the bag made it to the top of the blower. Nielson hit the release button, as quick as it had sucked up the leaves it released them into the dumpster they almost filled it.

Nielson had sucked up ¼ of the leafs on the ground in 2 hours that meant in 10 hours every leaf on the ground that was taking him 2 weeks to suck up had gave him 8 hours of work and 40 rows of vegetables, of every kind. Nielson gave the keys to his son you try it.

Pat turned the key to on position. He liked the sound of the engine a little rugged, but that was okay, it meant it was high powered.

Nielson raked at least in more rows less than Pat, Pat was younger and faster, and stronger not that it mattered it was how he took the turns that gave him a 4 row advantage.

The Chase

MARY O'DONALD LIKED WATCHING HORSE and dog races. Once in a-while she would bet $50.00 trifecta on horse races, o $50. a dog would end race at 3rd 2nd or 1st place.

She has been to a couple training sessions. She thought it was odd that the training for both was similar.

For example a dog was trained by a stuffed bunny tied to a pole. The dog ran after the bunny but never seemed to catch the rabbit. The horses training was a carrot or a piece of celery or some other hard vegetable, also tied to a pole, except the horse was not chasing a rabbit for the sport of it at least the horse did not think. So he was chasing it because he was hungry.

Once a horse or dog learned the faster it went more was he given to eat.

After going around a track (race) for a short year both the dog & the horse knew it was to run as fast as he. She could around a track whenever the dog or horse saw a horse or rabbit it thought of chasing the rabbit or chasing after vegetables for food.

Mary had been talking to a trainer or two about her buying a race horse or dog. He said he dealt with both race horse and dog. Surprising enough the dog races brought in much more money.

Mary decided to go with the dog. She could keep it in the house and not have to pay a housing fee. It would be like a pet dog that new how to race, lightning; flashing across the sky. The dog she named lightning it also reminded her of lightning streaking across the ski.

Lightning was happy with his name he thought it fit him. Streak did not think it was a dog's name but; that was the name he was given so he accepted it.

Sometimes Streak would visit his horse friend Lightning he would spend the night with him. If he got tired of visiting Lightning the base was across the lot. Streak and Lightning both had retired from the racing game. They became farm animals on Mary's farm.

Mary would hitch a wagon on Lightning and ride around the farm. Streak would follow. Mary sometimes would have a worker at the farm saddle up Lightning and they would go for a ride around the farm. Sometimes she would ride down an old dirt road that lead to an old school friend's house. While there they would play a game they played when they were young children. Her friends name was Hidie. The game they played was Knock, Knock. One would knock on a door. The other had to guess where the other one was; then they would run from one another and hide behind a door when music from an old RCA radio quite. Then hide behind door the one not behind a door when music stopped would have to guess behind what door was the other. Once they were found they would have to treat the other with a handful of candy. Baby size candy bars.

After eating the candy bar the chase would begin again.

Mary sometimes would let her friend catch her so they could get the candy and share it with each other.

They repeated it until all the candy was gone. Whoever was left outside had to go and buy more candy.

Mary was glad she had returned home to the farm, her chores were getting piled up.

Some dishes were piled in the sink. She scrapped the dried food off them then, soaked them in hot soapy water.

Ran a wash rag over them; or sponge them rinsed it off with hot water. If a towel was around used it to dry of plates if not left them to drip dry in a plate rack.

If you go to Mary's you can find the horse standing by the barn and he dog sleeping in the barn.

P.S. The new young puppy & young horse chase one another all around the farm.

Nitro Project

ONNIE WORKED FOR A MARKETING firm in Tulsa Oklahoma. He
was a physicist of microscopic fungi that makes up food particles
for frozen foods.

Donnie's job was being a taster of processed foods made by Nitro a
food for the future.

On the 19th of Jan he would be testing and sampling frozen foods
made by Nitro.

The Nitro Company decided to name the project they were working
on after the company.

Nitro was the name of a project the company was working on. It was
called the Nitro Experience, the food company had already figured food
could be frozen, over a period of time. The thing about Nitro frozen foods
it could be frozen quicker thru a process called Nitro freezing. The name
implies it is fast frozen.

At times the food being frozen was frozen too quickly and would cause
spoiling of the food by osmosis.

Nitro went to his lab he had a high powerful micrometer that could see
tiny microbs it could detect seriousness of the disease carrying microscopic
microbs. Most of the disease microbes comes from other microbs that has
been infected.

The Nitro Project lasted 5 years when a sudden stop came from
microbes infecting tools. Donnie could not believe what he was hearing.
All those years of his studies of microbes; out the window.

Donnie had to retreat to basics starting from sub zero-neg & poss-just
like on a car battery left neg richt pos. past. And like a car battery crossing
one with the other shorts out the system, if lucky it has not been damaged
too much.

Donnie preforms a series of test when he gets results from test that are pos. reading. He quickly advances to the next testing stage, hardly ever retreating to the past Nar to the present problems his interest was in future problems.

Donnie spent the night reading about problems at his shop and how he could not fix them.

After reading a couple chapters Donnie learned all he needed to and had moved on to the next chapter.

Chapter 4 was more specific the first 3 chapters were a little visive when it came to instruction it did not have detailed information.

The Package

JOYCE PAULEY WAS A PACKER at the Cornwall Packing Company. She worked on Line 14. Packing wool jackets and wool sweaters, Joyce opened up a 2x5 packing box it said for a blue and white sweater size 10, 6 inch sleeve.

There was a stack of blue wool sweaters laying on a dresser. Joyce picked up one sweater she played it down, folded the arms inwards towards the center. Then she folded it length wise in half; her third fold was from bottom to top then a role. She put it in a tube container screwed down the lid tight as she could. Addressed it then put a stamp on sent it on its way down a round tubular shoot. It landed in a grey cart. The cart was pushed to the out box door where it was put in a mail truck marked Hollywood.

Joyce chose a yellow and blue pair of slacks folded it over twice then put it in a second tubular container where it landed in the same cart as the sweaters both sweater and slacks had a code number matching so both would reach a person who also had the same code #. The three coded match was what for 8 hours at Joyce matched sweater, slacks and codes to get a gift to the person it was attended to go to for.

Joyce did not always work on the 3 code line. When no orders for sweater Joyce worked on line 37 packing and unpacking. The packages was already matched at Joyce had to do was either put a package in a box or take one that had been returned out of the box. When there was no shipments out or coming in. Joyce changed her job description again. Either back to packer, unpacker folder it was to keep her busy.

Sometimes Joyce was asked to do overtime at time and a half for 4 hours, bed of life a days week of 8 hours.

Usually she worked in a different area sometimes different building when working overtime hours.

Joyce had been working a steady number of hours 14 a day. She had gotten use to the 14 hours a day. A drop in orders caused a cut back in Joyce's hours. She need that lost time to pay some bills. Joyce looked for a second job. A grocery store on the west and was herein part timers for the next 3 month; by that time Joyce hopped to be back to her regular hours at her regular job. At the grocery she was also a packer. Joyce began to buy Christmas presents even though it was October, she had them in a closet in the basement closet.

Two weeks before Christmas Joyce was called back to work; her employers business picked back up. She kept the grocery store job for 16 hours a week then her total weekly hours was 24 a wk. Joyce reported to line 14 a new line for her. Still it was packaging. Her boss was pleased he did not need to retrain her. That saved him money and put her back to work sooner so she could get back to making some money for herself.

Joyce had 2 hours before reporting to her second job. Enough time to go home and freshen up before starting.

The evening went quick Joyce was on her way home to take a quick shower then off to bed. It would be 10:00 PM she would wake at 6:00 to get ready for her regular work starting at 8: AM.

Joyce had a work uniform she would need to put it in the washer and dryer before going to bed.

Joyce put on her freshly clean clothing sipped down some coffee then headed out the door. She arrived at work 10 minutes early. Just enough time for one more coffee before starting her shift at the packing company.

Kristin Duck and the Gecko

ONE MORNING KRISTIN DUCK WAS flying North to meet some other ducks and fly together in a pack of 50 or so.

She was all alone when she spotted a tiny creature running; standing up right. It was a male as far as she could tell. It had large (for its tiny size) black as coal eyes. It's back was a dark green and its front side white as snow.

It was a Gecko running to the meadow to catch a perch for its dinner. It was running because Kristin saw a perch jumping out of the river. As quickly as she could she spread her yellow and blue wings; then began flapping them. Her chest of green appeared up like a color like no other on her body.

With her strongest thrust Kristin rose up off the ground one foot; two foot three foot; then higher and higher until she was 45 feet up in the sky. When Kristin got to the level of 45 foot she saw the biggest perch she had ever seen. It look from the height she was flying to be 5 and a half feet from its nose to its tail fins.

Kristin nose dived and with one reach pulled the perch from the water.

One, two, three gulps and she had swallowed the perch until it was no more, after devouring the perch she followed the river upstream.

Kristin flew on; not yet meeting with another duck; not even of her kind. Once time she saw some geese flying north. She rushed to join them but by the time she had flown 20 feet they had vanished out of sight. Kristin thought she might be a little to west and turned to the east; where she saw some hawks making a meal out of a buffalo for fear that the hawks would attack her she kept her.

Kristin changed her course back to the north. After the hawks & buffalos she hoped there would be some kind of ducks flying north as she flew.

Another body of water came into focus. She could not tell but there was something drinking from it. She hopped to see a second animal approach the body of water. It did not resemble a bird of prey or even a bird at all. It was something with a 4 or 5 foot body, and arms at least 2 foot in length before its hand which had 1½ inch length. Kristin time to reach the northern lake was getting short before the snows of the north began. It had already gotten cold and she expected colder weather ahead.

Kristin was getting hungry she started scanning both the land and any body of water she flew over for a bite to eat.

Once again she came by a creature that was similar to the creature that was 4 or 5 foot body. I was also similar in length to the one she had seen early. Its colors also green, yellow and; blue.

Kristin flew to the ground closer it began to take shape. It was no longer standing upright. It was like a python slithering on the ground towards the body of water.

Kristin could now tell what the body of water was. I was a stream flowing backwards. Instead of flowing from the north to the south or east to west. The flow was upstream from the south to north.

The green yellow and blue creature on its feet was crawling on its stomach in a northerly upstream Kristin still in search of other ducks flying in a north western or north eastern direction had not yet found any other ducks. She was the only duck in any airspace she had been flying in.

Kristin flew closer to the creature and closer to the ground to examine the creature more.

She landed 2 foot from it. The creature shook with fear the Kristin was going to eat it.

She had no such thought to her it was an odd looking and never had she seen Kristin went closer the creature was on its stomach the slithering as a snake on the prowl. The creature headed Kristin's direction as she went towards it the creature come towards her. Closer & closer they came to one another. Eye ball to eye ball they stood neither moving an inch both their eyes rotating up & down, side to side. Each one expecting the other to attack. After a few brief moments both turned and went back the way they came.

Kristin took to the sky in a northerly direction. The creature headed in an east southern direction. Neither to see one another again.

What was it Kristin had such a meeting with? She knew not and went her own way.

The creature Kristin had meet up with was a Gecko. They never had introduced themselves nor had they meet again.

Black Stone

S HELLY COMBES LIKED HORSE RACING; since she was 9 years of age. Back then 1981 she would go to Pemblico Race Track, Kentucky Derby, Alga Rose and when passable Lexiton and Turfway. None on the same cercute.

Shelly has won in total of all her racing connections a total of $3,000,000.90. One evening Shelly was watching the Lexington Raceway. When she saw a horse that came from 21st place all the way to 5th in a matter of .53 seconds. The horse never made it above 4th place winning ¼ of the purse.

Shelly quickly called her agent Leroy. She told him of the horse 1 what is his name the agent asked and in "what race or race track did?" Shelly in reply it was the 5th of July at Lexington race track in Lexington Kentucky.

What impresses you about this horse? The agent asked. Its beautiful black color and the quickness it came from 21st place to 5th I have to have this magnificent horse. Shelly buys horses from owners who had a horse win a major race. Okay. Give me the horse's name "His name is Black Stone!" Shelly replied to her agent.

"Your" "in luck" "I know of that horse and its history quickness is one of his traits his fault the owner has never been able to get a major horse racing contract. The owner is Ted Blackstone, the horse is named after himself. "I'll give him a call this Friday" Shelly call you back 2 weeks. Shelly had waited 2 weeks then returned a call to her agent. She inquired about Black Stone. "We are in deliberation. I will be meeting him in 2 days and at that time I'll make an offer, and keep raising it until he sells me the horse you call Black Stone.

Shelly waited for the letter for 2 weeks. He had bought Black Stone for $12.4 million after a rundown on the horse's history at each track he ran.

I was an impressive run. He was rated by the Horse Racing Association as the 8th highest earnings made.

That was before his last race at Pemblico. Black Stone only 3 years old could race 3 or 4 more years.

Black Stone arrived on the Combs Horse Corals on March of 2001. Shelly had made a separate stall for Black Stone. She did not buy him for racing she bought him for show.

Black Stone has long legs and his stride is less, between each outstretch allowing him to cover more ground quicker therefore reaching finish line 3 or 4 horse lengths.

After a quick clean up and brushing Black Stone was ready for his first showing.

On Nov 21 a showing of horses where first place won a purse of 9 sherry centered Black Stone in the showing of breed's competition. Black Stone was given a number 21 commemorating his first race of overcoming a multiple of horses. Black Stone took his place on display showcase 21. It was shortly when the first group entered a panel of 12 mixed female and male show horses. Black Stone the only horse to have raced the score 11-08-for Black Stone the next showing in another place the score was 19-4 Black Stone over all. Black Stone had a score of 30-12 enough for a first place. Shelly quite racing and followed up on her career as a Show Agent for horses that were entered in a horse showing competition Black Stone retired from both racing and showing lived in his own style of stall.

Arie'o and Mr Seals

ARIE'O LIVED AT THE OCEAN floor; in a house of wet gewee sand. It was outside of the dark caverns on the top of the ocean floor.

The place where Mr. Seals resided a deep dark place that had money caverns.

Passage ways made their way in all direction in and out of caverns pitch dark. Mr. Seals had no problem with the darkness. He was a bat owl. Like a bat a bat out could find its way around in black dark places.

A bat owl also has long razor sharp claws that gives him a sturdy grip on the dark cavern walls. His razor sharp claws helps him chop up foods that he scoops up from the watery cavern floors. Arie'o swims above the floors of the watching that the natural flow of the ocean and its creations and flow in its intended course.

Arie'o is a life game of the ocean's floor. A job she appreciates and is happy to do. Mr. Seals also a seeper of the caverns on the ocean floors caverns; passage ways and tunnels.

Arie'o was watching over some blow fish. When one went off from the other. Arie'o could not follow both, she when ones size shrank to small proportion.

The smaller much easier to follow Arie'o was her choice to look after, she would leave the bigger to Mr Seals.

Arie'o saw the smaller being attacked by electric seal. Arie'o quickly made her appearance visible to the electric seal. When the seal saw her it reversed its course and swam off in the opposite direction.

A close call Arie'o thought as she swam. As she went on her way.

Mr. Seals had the same experience in the passage ways of the dark caverns. One of the baby bat owls wondered off. Mr. Seals searched for a couple hours he was about to quit searching when he herd a little squeak.

It was the baby bat. It was stuck between to thin walls inside the dark cavern walls.

Mr. Seals flew to the thin walls and pecked away until the walls crumbled and freed the baby owl from the clutches of the narrow walls.

Arie'o and Mr. Seals freed from the walls grab; the baby bat owl, landed outside from the baby bat owl caverns.

Mr. Seals was happy he was able to set free to baby bat owl.

Mr. Seals flew back to the dark cavern and searched around looking for dangers that might have put other baby bat owls in danger.

Arie'o had just left the outer walls of the caverns. She was free flying. The area she was flying in was free of dangers. So Arie'o relaxed a bit and took time out to free fly around in the not so dark caverns.

Arie'o and Mr. Seals meet outside and together both fly freely together.

Mr. Seal's spot's a mouse on the ground a good meal for the bat owls. He dives quickly and captures it in his sharp claws and together they have a tasty meal together.

After the meal Mr. Seals flies back to the inside of the caverns. Arie'o flies home where she arrives in time for an afternoon nap before going out and search for her evening.

Arie'o strikes out and only catches a small mouse before she retires for the night, when the sun rises the next day Arie'o and Mr. Seals take flight together in search for their breakfast meal together just as they do every morning.

Took into the southern skies you may see Arie'o and Mr. Seals searching for breakfast.

The Rivers Bend

THE RIVER IN TULSA VALLEY carves about 15° West towards the Gulf of Mexico. About 6 miles of sandy beaches reveals a fisherman's paradise approaching a flat top hotel painted green in one side black around the corner and unknown from the south land view of the river of the two northern sides, unless you cross over and view the western view shows a large heavy wood brown tree approx. 50 foot high, 6 foot from bottom land a square hole from the front to the house. Two windows on the left two to the right one left is 3 foot from ground level to the right of the tree one on right 3 foot ground level on the side painted black a door about 7 foot high 7 foot wide" red door looking perhaps from a helicopter or plain the roof paint red seems to have a bench on rivers side middle of ceiling a bench running front to back of the building or what appears to be front. Looking from front the building unleased in side length. Tilting the building outward towards the river.

What appears to be a sandy beach starts off from the west with spurts of long grass blades rising from the sand, where the river meets the land. Looks of a boat dock, black and brown in color. As the river extend its width appears to be around 30 foot or perhaps 50 foot mountains brown in color rises and lowers from west to east. Above the mountains a light blue ski peering across the length of the river. In the ski further in the sky seems to be dark black rain clouds with rain drops coming out of them, back across the river about 13 foot land side to river appears to be a floating dock. Ceiling of red frontal area brown with black rimbed windows. A door 3 windows painted black on the ward to the southward on land dark brown strips and light brown sand midway stand a man with a pail blue shirt light brown corduroy pants appear to be looking towards river. As the river bend in land a sliding dock pulled inland on side of sliding dock seems to be a night club or a storage area the frontal view showing a parking area unmarked eastward in river 2 foot from inland a paddle boat makes it way upstream land in splotches with a 3 story house on left an oak tree almost to top of 3 story house north inland a tree 5 foot high eastward a black hawk seems to be caring a fish it pulled out of water, blue sky stretching upwards and east at land level what seems to be a island with black tree trunks suggesting maybe a pure at one time as you looking towards the river and island 2 small dingy or perhaps a porty boat heads same direction as the paddle boat, the river bends south a black man stands at the bend going south inland a cabin light brown green doors now approaching near the river another man light green short fishes in river about ½ mile from the rivers bend. In the skyline a dark black closed to the left towards river a large beak bird perhaps a duck.

The rivers bend suggest there is hardly any activity around the bend not even that of a snake or worm perhaps aunts or crabs but no trades appear.

It is said fish are plenty because no fishing activity around the rivers bend not just one species. Bass, polk, tuna and perch all pass on their journey north. Come winters break.

It would seem that at one time or the other a fisherman might stand at the rivers bend and fish since the fish on their way north to spawn are so many different species that pass the rivers bend.

Jerry's Pad

HAD PAID OF HIS HOUSE it was in his name as the owner. Jerry decided to remodel the old house. It was all banged up. On the inside, the kitchen tiles were cracked apart, the living room rags are torn, and a ball of twine strung across the bedroom.

In Jerry's master bedroom curtains hung with holes all around. Wall of carbon board ripped from studs it had been nailed too.

Jerry began his remodeling in the back room where the water cooler was. Jerry the water cooler was running slow and sluggish.

Jerry bought a new Sears water cooler after unhooking the old water cooler. Jerry set in the new Sears water heater that had more features than the old. Set me a temp gauge; water level gauge and a steam release valve. About an hour's work.

After replacing the water cooler Jerry went to the dry and washer. The dryer's door was coming off the hinges it was on. The washer hot & cold valve sometimes did not work. Jerry's total time of repairs was 5 hours to utility room appliances and walls. Plus curtains.

Jerry had to rebuild his funds before starting on the dining area next. The dinner seat paint peeling from legs all around. Jerry went out and bought some stripper with a number a paint bristle brush and razor blades to cut away chipped wood in hard to get to places after cutting away old paint. Jerry ended up repairing 5 of 8 rooms the cost of $2,875.50. Jerry had added a card or game room with the latest updated computers. Jerry's Pad is always open people can work on the new technology available on the super computer, he has installed on his computer game room.

They also play non computer games like card packer and solitaire. They can just set on one of his recliners or the folding up couch, and relax a while before the attempt to tackle another game or build another program.

Jerry's Pad is also full of great eating snacks wise baby dogs rolled in maple leaf bacon. If muscle cramps two swimming pools with rotating waves to work out soreness after a relaxing stage one might pies threw one of the pads many telescopes and cheek out the star constellations or watch a meteor dropout of the sky.

Jerry advanced his home 3 times over. It is a much more fun place and people pleasing place. The added rooms makes sleeping rooms when converted.

Jerry is always in house greeting patrons into the pad.

The first sight when entered Jerry's Pad is a pina colota shaped like a giant star. Two the right a wall of games on play stations google play system spectrum and blink system as you go further in a Chinese food dinner with Chow Main noodles chicken fry and rice to the left a Japanese setting with Japanese flags & American flags. Jello and puckling served in tiny plates with lettuce leaves surrounding the jello and the puddrige at the back was another display Jerry's collection of apple and lemon meringue pies.

The last place you would be before leaving to go to the assigned bed.

Jerry was first to use and called guest out for the morning breakfast.

People came to see the Jerry's Pad and their interest in the pad assured there would be more visitors.

The Long Road Home

CARL MOORE WAS DISCHARGED FROM military in 1981. From Fort Summit Alabama after a 25 year career.

Starting out as an enlisted soldier of no ran. As did many young soldiers did when entering military. Staying as an enlisted until a month after his first year.

On Jan 17 1988 enlisted man Carl Moore was promoted to Corporal. Then after 6 months he was promoted again to Sargent E-1 on September 2001 he reached the rank of E-5 Sargent fifth place. He was given charge of a Carl's re-enlistment was coming he had to make a decision. Re-enlist or civilian life? He thought about re-enlisting he would get a re-enlistment bonus plus a promotion to E-6 another but as freedom from military life he choose to be a civilian. It would be a chance he would not regret Carl handed in his uniforms dress greens; his jungle camouflaged combat cloths. He would change them for a pair of blue slacks that rolled up and no authority. It would probably take a month or two to get a title. Carl decided to take the chance of becoming a self-employed owner of his own bossiness. He was quite knowledgeable in mechanics. The military gave him a retirement check of 21,000.00. That would get him a start. He did not like being in military anyway.

After a month Carl bought some land. The next month he began building his garage. His first customer was an old friend Chester Bloom. Chester owned a 2001 Courger. It had a blown engine. Carl rebuilt the engine, since Chester was an old buddy Carl charged him only for parts. Chester thank Carl for his kindness then shave away.

It was 4 month until evil had another customer. He was losing money. Carl sold the business, and looked around for another, he was a pretty good salesman; a damp-any was developing across town. It was still in the car industry. Selling tires for rethreads. After selling retreads for a month Carl decided that was not his calling either. For the next year Carl wondered from one job to another. Striking out on everything he tried.

One evening he was on his journey home when he saw Mark Sweeny working in the fields; planting veggies; corn; tomatoes; potatoes; pepper and Carl went to Marks. He saw Mark was shorthanded Carl offered his services on the farm. Mr. Sweeny did need the help but what difference would one person make?

Three days later Carl was planting baby red tomatoes and broccoli and others like green beans, sweat corn even rice.

Carl was offered life work on the Sweeny Farm. It had been 5 long years of searching for his calling. Little did he know it was working on a farm in quarters he had worked as a 13 year old boy.

Carl became a full time farmer at the Sweeny's farm. He became special caretaker and salesperson for Sweeny Foods.

Control of the Blue Ash Eagles

IT WAS A STRONG WINDY day Sept 29th 2001. When a flock of eagles of 13,500 flew into Blue Ash.

There was no room for human and eagles. Blue Ash not a gigantic town, less people than the eagles that had been blown in from the strong heavy winds.

The heavy strong winds was not letting up grounding the Blue Ash eagles. A name they were given by Blue Ash Residence. Blue Ashes Mayor was consulting with other mayors about the situation of the eagles being grounded by the heavy preparation. The winds have not diminished enough for the eagles to take flight and go elsewhere. They are at least flocking to the mountain side of Blue Ash.

Their population is setting bigger they have mated some having 3 or 4 siblings.

The mayors all agree something has to be done. Maybe crotting them up then shipping them elsewhere. If not that building them a sanctuary?

The winds have diminished the eagles has made homes in Blue Ash for the families they have given life too.

Control seems to be the operative. Since the mayor or anyone else can think of another solution to the over population of the Blue Ash eagles. The mayor still searching for funds to ship at least a quarter of them even shipping of ¼ of the Blue Ash eagles would prove to be expensive. The mayor suggest that the conservator & crotting some off might relieve the over population. Some have suggested killing them for meals would be of some help? But that could not give a permanent population control of the eagles. With this new scenario might relieve the problem enough to where the problem has worn down a little. The mayor has crews working day and night structuring crates to ship them away. A fifth scenario where do the

Blue Ash eagles get moved to? No one has any idea where they originated from. Some place in the south west seems to be how they migrated to Blue Ash. Some have gone back to the south west, seems to be a natural environment for the eagles.

It has been 6 month since the Blue Ash eagles has landed any recognition as of their inheritance. The mayor completed the conservatory and left it up to the eagles choose to stay or search the ski since the numbers has diminished the mayor suggest that in time the situation to the overpopulation of this large beautiful bird will seek it origins and the eagles will began in number only leaving those who choose to stay would.

Since the eagle has left in such great quantities. Those that remain are welcomed, the add not just a great beauty to the town (city) of Blue Ash but an attraction by followers of the great bird and that helps the community by taxes raised on antiques sold to visitors.

Black Tide

THE SKY OH SO BLUE early in the morning. The sky shines bright and blue, a clear blue sky shines all day long.

The sun shines through the bright blue sky. The sky so blue shines for you and I in the twilight hours. So beautiful of a sky that opens the gates of heaven for you and I. The sky so blue turns to a darker blue then a misty the days linger into the gray of the evening then to the pitch black night for one second then a twinkle in the black sky then another twinkle then all across the sky twinkles the stars of the black tide.

The black tide opens up the night time and the twinkling of the stars brightens the black tide. Exposing things that move around during the black night.

The black tide is not of the day lights bright and beautiful sky.

The black night is that of the sleeping and the wanderers that roam around during the black tide the black night is for those who are quick to scatter. Those who can catch a falling star quicker than batting an eye. During the very short moments of the dark tide, the dark tide a space between daylight hours of the blue ski. A starless space with no light, a space where everything lay still a space that connects the day light hours with the evening, a space where hardly anything occupies.

The black tide is like sleep everything out of connection nothing moves in the black tide. It is a place where nothing is. A large area of blackness that less between the blue skies of the day and the twilight of the night sky.

The black tide is not for the young. They fumble around for it is too dark to make things out in their young undeveloped eye sight. It is not for the old whose sight has diminished the black tide is a vacancy area where no oxygen exist, where only motorized power is engaged so an object can pass through on its journey elsewhere.

A place where if such a vehicle was to falter it would drift around in the black tide.

The black tide never waves one way or the other. It is always still. Not even if it is pushed will the black tide shift between the blue sky on the late evenings of the twilight.

The black tide is like a table setting in a room with chairs pushed in all the way, until a force passes into the black tide. The motorized vehicle moves the last that has been still and not moved a inch since being captured by the black tide; with a force of minor power a last object is pushed into the daylight hours of the blue sky or into the late evenings twilight.

The black tide sets idol between the daylight hours the black tide is a resting place for that which has been pushed into it. A place where objects remain frozen in time; and is not released until a vehicle pushes it forward or backwards or from beneath it pushing it upwards; atop forcing the item downward. The black tide is for nothing of life or substance it is meant to be just as it is a black empty space between the sunny daylight hours and the twinkling late evening hours. So as not to confuse the black tide with a black hole; objects drift into a black hole and exit in another galaxy the black tide is a mass of stiff mater that remains still until forced to move. Like a person pulling a chair from under a table the chair shift one place to the other.

My Buddie

JUST SETTING AT MY KITCHEN table looking out one of my windows; I see a dog running across my back yard. With my sharp eyes I follow it. It passes the storage area I had made for storing gardening tool. I notice its color. It was a mix of light brown and medium color of brown its face was black with a nose almost as wide as its face. The rest of its body was a light brown. Curious about why it was running I went out the kitchen door

Looking to the, the way it was running I saw why the dog was running. It was chasing a rabbit. While I was watching the rabbit look a stay right, the dog kept running in the direction that he and the rabbit running. He notices the rabbit had taken a right; then glides to a stop quickly he reverses his direction and goes back to where the rabbit had changed his to the right. He runs across my neighbor's yard; then his neighbor's yard. By this time the rabbit had ran across two yards and was slowing down because the dog was out of his sight. The dog I had figured was a rat killer. He had finally got tired of chasing the rabbit. He changed his course to where he had first started chasing the rabbit.

I notice the dog is panting from his run. I fill a bowl full of water and take it to him. He begins drinking it with his long pink tongue.

Bully is the name I decided to give him. He has no dog collar on. I figure he is a stray wondering dog.

Bully lays down at my feet to rest from that fast long run. I reach down to pet him. His tail wags. I open my back door and Bully steps through it into the kitchen Bully looks around he sees the refrigerator. "Oh" maybe Bull is someone's dog he knows that the frig has food in it, I open it. Bully uses his right paw and pulls out the bottom rack. On it I have a cooked piece of honey ham; a bowl of beets; a half loaf bread; and a German baloney. I slice of same of the German baloney; about 2 inch thick and the same in width a square piece.

Bully grabs it with his sharp pointing teeth.

Bully eats half then looks around he sees a crack in the lower bottom dining area wall. He hides the rest of the German baloney in the crack, then goes over to the water bowl and lays down. I have come to the conclusion Bully has decided he will stay 'I'm glad Bully falls asleep and I go to the fridge and take out the honey ham, open a box of macaroni and broccoli. It takes about half an hour to fix dinner and set it on the table. Bully wakes from his slumber. He smells the honey ham and macaroni. I have cookie. His tail begins to waggle and he jumps up and down I've seen dogs do this before he wants some of the food I have made.

I think that is only fair I have wanted him to be my doggie friend, and he has decided to be my human friend. I decide to teach him some tricky I have a tennis ball in the closet; I play tennis once in a while with Daniel a friend of mine. I toss it across the room stage. He know to chase it and bring it back. That affirms he must be owned by someone I put a add in paper for a month no one claims him and he is getting use to the name I gave him. I gave up on looking for a person to claim him. He does not mind that his over has not cooked for him. I decide to teach him a second trick setting up. I use a doggie biscuit. I put it on the floor then bring it to my chest. Bully stands up and begs; another sign he had an owner; I wonder how many tricks he knows I try a couple more I know. Bully know them all.

Whoever his owner was took the time to train him with have liked him. I decide to put a second add in paper. 2 more weeks Bully has been outside a lot he has had a chance to go back to who ever his owner was but makes no effort to.

A year passes by this time I figure Bully is my dog. And Bully must figure he and I are buddies.

Bully has learned to open the screen door and I have cut out a doggie door; so he can come and go as he pleases I have retired and I also come and go as I please. Sometimes Buddy goes with me he follow right behind me. Everyone that passes pets him on the head. I don't mind and neither does he.

Everywhere I go I take Bully with me. When he wants to go for a walk he grabs his leach leather and we go for a walk. While at home Bully and I play. It runs in the other room then back towards me the jumps up on chest knocking me down then he kisses me.

Bull and I are not only buddies but we are best of buddies.

The Girl with The RV's

S HANNON STINE SAVED $1,500.00 SHE took it to the car sales on the eastern part of town. It was full of used cars under $2,000.00.

Shannon went down the rows of cars on the lot. A car was not her interest too small even the largest car. An old station wagon maybe. After taking inventory, she decided station wagon was too small also Desoto wagon also too small. She needed a van, a lot of empty space in a van. Room to store packages but not quite enough, she needed more vacant room. The packages she was going to deliver were large she wanted to get more than 24 packages in the mobile unit she was going to delivery with.

There was only one choice left. The R.V. It was wider and longer than most vehicles. It could carry more packages. In the packages was medical supplies, also she delivered medical beds.

Shannon would go out and look at R.V.'s after looking at 10 she choose the one with the most inside room she measured each one as she looked at it. Shannon raid for the RV with cash. Shannon contacted hospitals, and had contracts to deliver medical supplies for them, she also contacted pharmacies, private and ones in hospitals. Shannon bought her second RV after 5 months of deliveries. She used one for east side & one for west. After 5 more month she used one north & one south. Shannon extended her RV's to grocery stores. She needed more she bought 4 more vans her total now was 15 vans. Not quite enough she bought 5 more to make her delivery service RVs a total of 20 vans.

She hired 40 people to deliver with one driver and the other relief driver for when driver got tired of driving. Shannon made a home base for the R.V. drivers to call in for direction to the delivery client rather home or hospital, or pharmacies. It was not long until Shannon had her radio in all vans and hospitals. They were also in pharmacies. Shannon's delivery service Shannon paid for the gas for the vans. The hospitals paid for oil and grease used to make things work right were paid by a mechanic who done all repair work on the 20 van's.

Shannon numbered the RV's so she would know which one was in repair. She had also bought a RV to fill in for a van that might have broken down. Shannon has gotten a call for medical supplies (first aid) she has the amount the customer is asking for but that will leave her with none, she ask the customer if she can order less, the customer says yes.

Shannon can now order the supplies she needs. Once a year different time for each RV. Shannon has the RV's cleaned, and an overhaul mechanical fixes and tire changes rim changes. Once a week she fills their tanks Shannon has created a reliable business and her clients can count on her and her RV's.

The Geese in The North West

EVERY MORNING WHEN I TAKE a walk to either the bank or +100 the family dollar; or office depot. If I'm early enough I see about 10 geese. There is no water around except what might be draining from a small creek behind the bushes over by the health food store I stop in west. I have taken pictures of them. I do not think they are always same geese. I'm going to see what kind of foods they eat. Then see if there is any on the ground between the fence or family dollar.

There has to be something drawing them to same spot year after year. Maybe it is the grass that grows by the fence? or seed from another animal or plant that also returns every year? I've looked on the ground I do not see any signs of anything. Maybe geese have a special scent from female and a male follows to mate? It is nice and sunny out. I think I'll take the bus to Locus; then to the bank. Tell the bank my visa card is missing and have them issue me new one for the 7th time. No charge for it they will issue a new one, if I do not have one cannot over draw nor can I put money in my account for visa card. Where I overdraw when I use it for a bill or to buy something with other than Chase Bank A.T.M.

Guess I'll take some more pictures of the geese. Still would like to know what brings them here year after year. Must be a migration thing. They are headed north and Salem Ave St Route 49 is in their path of flight. Don't see why? Just a landing place to rest I guess anyway they are pretty looking birds especially when the spread their wings. Once in a while. The will fight turnaround one another. And sometimes they just sit around for a while then take for the air four or five at a time then spread their wings out flap then a couple times then glide for about a mile or so. Never have seen more than 10 or 12 at a time some birds fly in flocks of 100 or 500.

Could be they join others on their way north, or maybe not. Maybe they just fly in.

I walk further north or south and see them in any other place and then only a few at a time. They might not even be family just a few geese that happen to land in same area, I've never seen them chase down another animal for their food. Nor have I seen any bird seed laying around on the ground. Guess they feed elsewhere perhaps a late further north or one to the south on their way up north or on their way back south. Maybe they are like Samon go north to spawn where there is hundreds of others of some kind.

Every year I take a picture and I'll sit on the fence rails between the office depot and family dollar. If I stay on 49 Kentucky Fried if I'm in the mood for chicken if I was a person who liked wild game I might buy a bow and arrow or a cross bow and shoot one for dinner. I hear they are good and juicy game. Also I hear they are clean birds taking a swim every chance they get or come across a body of water. Their food chain is healthy. Mostly fruit and wheat. They may stop to eat.

Beaver Mountain

JOHNY WINSTON WAS A LOGGER by trade. He had 4 different axe blades for light work. For heavy work he had battery operated saws Johny had inherited his father's saw mill. There were all kinds of trees that were planted in rows of some kind.

The acreage the saw mill had was 976 or so not over 1000 acres. There were oak pine spruce maple and many others that also grew on this acreage was 12 lakes. Ten streams and 4 ponds. They were placed on the land so water would be available for all the trees that was close by. The water pond lake streams were all shared with wild life.

Mr. Winston thought that wild life had as much right to the water as any human.

After all animals is one of human's food services. Johny had an order for some apple not a tree used normally for building things. The order was for 102 cords, when the person who was ordering called Johny what sort of thing was he was using apple to build with the customer said he was grinding some apple and cedar together cedar would give it long jeverty and apple would make it have a pleasant odor. Johny went to the apple trees he had planted. Any particular flavor, or kind, like winter grove green red or brown apple look? The customer thought for a while and chose wine sap and some Washington, you're in luck I have both

Johny put his chain saw in the back of his 1969 Chevy duce and a half Johny was a collector of trucks.

While Johny was cutting on a cedar tree he saw Beaver chopping down a small cedar. He did not mind as long as they did not clog up the streams or lakes. Some of the damns Beavers made directed water flow trees Johny was growing that was a good thing then Johny need not spend a lot of money on a large sprinkling system. The Beavers lived not in the valley where the logging camp were but high in the mountains where there was a great lake that ran over the mountains edges and into the valley below giving a water source for the trees that grew on Johny's logging camp.

Beavers were busy every day making dams so their homes would not flow downstream especially in the winter when Beaver knead down a tree house and their it was no problem when they nawed down a bunch it created dry area's at the logging camp. That was not so good.

When a lot of Beavers chopped down trees Johny had to get certain trees elsewhere. Making a spendature for the logging camp and creating a deficit on the logging accounting books. Miscellaneous on deficit sheet was a deficit also. Johny was running a business and businesses were for profit not for money out that created a deficit.

Even though the Beavers were a problem they also were helpful in providing water ways to trees Johny was growing for profit.

Some of the residence thought it would be a good name for the occupants that lived atop the mountain or even on the way to the top the look a vote and Beaver Mountain won 75 percent of the rate majority vote. The Mountains were named Beaver Mountain when a person herd Beaver Mountain you knew he was headed up the mountain either for camping or visit the lodge that took on the Beaver name of Beaver Lodge making a suggestion that anyone in the Beaver Mountains was welcome to stay at the lodge; instead of camping among bugs or wild creatures that also lived on Beaver Mountain; like bears wolfs coyotes wild dogs or wild cats such as cougars tigers or mountain lions; that was the biggest of all the wild animals on the mountain.

As years passed Beaver Mountain grew people and wild life learned to live together until the hunter came to Beaver Mountain the trapped the Beavers and used then for pets (coats for winter wear).

The Timer as A Tool

In my kitchen, I have a timer I sometimes use to time cakes and other baking task. I decide to take on. Like I have never made a pot pie. Pretty simple cooking job. I've just never have made one.

Well when my wife's insurance check get hear I'm going to buy. Flower and egg a milk. Make a dough add some soda baking powder or yeast preferably yeast something that will get it to rise not much just life dough on a pie does.

Using the timer as a tool I've used a timer for other kinds of jobs besides cooking set a time to wake up when no duck was around and timer was. Used times when had a set time to be somewhere set it earlier than time of approval. Used a timer to time a job I was doing. Timed a 3 minute egg.

Used timer for exercising when time was stated.

The timer to me is a reminder that it is time to do something. If timer has more than an hour; I set another to go off before an hour latter. The most useful thing I've used the timer with is cooking especially if it is baking a pie; a cake; a pot pie, baritoe a timer can be used as a set time to stop a certain action, it can be used to a begin an action. Or to stop an action between given times.

Timing an action between time of begin to end. If only you are to sleep slumber for an hour a timer would be a tool to wake you up in an hour or less.

I am going to store taking the timer with me at least I will know how long by walking it is going to take me to reach my destination. Might as well time my self-coming home, what I really want is took now how for the distance is to my destination? If I reach it in an hour I think it might be 2 or 3 miles maybe 4 no more. I'll finish this when I return. Taking timer with me. Each time it goes off an hour once I figure out miles per hour then I will know the total mileage. From my apartment to the pharmacy, health store where my lady friends work. I take walks their visit them for an hour or two then come home. Then stop at the family well I went to store the lady who was going to make me a bracelet gave me back my $30.00 because she could not make it less than $100.00 the deal was $50.00. I had paid her $30.00.

The timer had gone off. It was the third ring on top their when I got home. The timer can be used as a metronome timing your string fingers from one to the other; giving you a better tone. The metronome is the instrument to use but if it is not available a timer can get your fingers on a given note when you need to strife the string. When playing with others your timers is to get you and a harmonizing voice when both on same note and hitting it at the time given.

The timer can help the tone of the note you are trying to hit in unison with others playing same note.

The timer can be thought of as a tuning fork that lets you know the string your hitting is coming along as it should. Can be you friend when tuning an instrument rather it be string or wood instrument know when to hit a certain note at the given time.

Susie Cruiser

J AMES & CATHY DOCKED THEIR river boat at Dales Landing $1000.00 a year. 8.33 a day-They also rented a cabin at the Lake Sanal price 7.33-16.66 a day which amounted to 16.66 x 7.=56.62 or $ 126.48 month, or 126.48 x 12 a year.

James & Cathy named their cruiser Susie Cruiser three or 4 times a week James & Cathy got in Susie Cruiser traveled down or upstream not always same direction depending on if they were fishing or just cruising mostly cruising. Fishing mostly on Friday Saturday or Sundays the weeks fishing depended on spawning of fish, and that was by the month of year certain fish spawned and the kind of fish they wanted to catch for eating. Other than fishing for food it was sport of it then they threw it back after catching it just to see if same fish was same one they had thrown back. If they were docked fish usually go upstream to spawn lay eggs then go back down stream catching one on rebound was rare. But has been done.

Traveling up stream was just as fun as downstream. A little harder because of water always blows downstream mostly even though a motor boat they turned off the motor and floated downstream. They only used motor to go Easter downstream and go upstream. When not on Susie Cruiser they were either fishing from bank or in cabin cooking fish they had caught. They had a television watched local shows, news mostly, and some of their favorite TV shows. They also had a radio on the console listened to sports & watched what games they could pack up. Most of the day they spent on business adventures.

James had a vacation coming, he accrued 3 weeks they spent two up north, parties mostly. James pulled the motor and starting the engine Cathy gathered up 7 poles 2 reel 4 casting rods one fly rod. It was her that liked fly fishing. James thought to much movement scare fish away, too much standing also. He liked setting & fishing again less movement fish did not scare away, James was a setter worked setting down, only time he stood even when he was steering the boat he set the control seat was at window level, and hands length.

Not mush fish activity for neither they agreed to change position move upstream where most fish spend their time spawning. Once fish born made more fish 15 or 20 a litter 10 made it to adult size. The cruiser went about 125 feet the river was still James figured not much fishing or boating going on then again might be a dry spot (no fish at all,)

James thought he would try it out. He threw a sinker into the water it did not go far there was string left; when it hit bottom shallow water James pulled the line up they went. James steered the cruiser upstream Cathy got some refreshments out of the mini refrigerator the opened some onion chips and Cathy got out some cheddar sour cream. The fishing poles tied down to a steak on side of boat. They set drinking soda eating chips and watching line.

James saw his line jerk he jumped up reeled in a 1 pound blue and yellow belly sunfish that was the only catch of the day, enough to feed the both of them with fried collie flower or hominy grits; or potatoes. James brought along a couple saterns. He pumped them up. Enough light to see the yellow string he was using it shown in the dark maybe they would catch those overnight. The total over night was 5. It was a better catch, Cathy put them in ice right after unhooking them they were frozen when they reached home. She put them in the home freezer. She had bought macaroni and cheese and creamed broccoli. They liked with fish dinners.

Cathy would make meatloaf when no fish were caught or ham & cheese sandwiches, Cathy & James took a day off fishing and spent the day shopping for supplies fishing gear, James bought night goggles he did a lot of night fishing. He also bought waxed worms colored lures and sinkers. Cathy bought bake in goods pie, and preserves and bread. James & Cathy had fished for 3 days; it would take 3 day get back home one day of rest then another day to restack fishing gear a second day restack boat. Then out for yet more fun on the river. All ready to go James and Cathy hoped on the cruiser, Jim pulled the cord and upstream then went headed for Dock 22, 18 miles away. At the 8 mile journey they stopped for a dinner lunch. ½ hour then back on the river for more fishing of the side of the cruiser. Susie baited her own line except for night crawlers and eel if they had it, she did not mind fish for bait, Susie Cruiser was well known on the rivers all around and at every port.

Time Well Spent

JANE AND LARRY WERE FRIENDS since they were 8 years of age. The lived across the street from one another. Both liked ice hockey. The watched their favorite team on Jade's portable television. Jade watched the goalie positions on every team he Larry was a fan of the line guards. He watched all the plays of every guard on every team. The Detroit Red Wings, the Washington Bluebirds and other teams. Jade adapted moves of every goal tender and Larry watched all the guards' moves, and adapted them. The also added them. They both joined the Red Wings their home team they lived in Detroit. On their off days they studied hockey moves, and practiced them. Jade and Larry became the best two team mates in hockey. There was not one move on still they did not know. This gave then an advantage over other hockey players. Together they reached the highest hockey honors more than once and held them the longest.

Jade & Larry also were equipment wise Jade had 8 specialty gloves he wore and each had a special purpose. Jade's gloves were to play the player more than the puck. Still he kept an eye on the puck as it slide on the ice towards the goal. At the player level he could estimate when a player was going to shoot for the goal by his stance and his height of the stick; he could tell what direction or angle the puck would be approaching the hockey net and when it would reach his goal. Once the puck was near enough he specked it as hard as he could mostly where he saw no players. Jade was so good he could send the puck sliding in between two players only inch apart. Jade Larry new the moves of any one who played hockey and they had played them so many times they knew what actions they would perform to get to the goal and shoot for a point. Jade and Larry's game is with Pittsburg-they have played the penguins 12 times in their career it is split 6-6-Detroit-has the advantage-going into the 7th game between them they are top hockey teams. Detroit's advantage is they are from the north lot of ice although it does get cold in Pittsburg and they have ice on their lakes also the determining factor maybe Detroit slightly colder weather. Both teams play inside & both play outside and the outside is much harder because of weather condition, wild animals and new & old grass, trees and weather change.

Both teams are always checking weather condition and both check condition of their arena's. Neither hesitate when it comes down to spending money to improve arena's inside & outside nor are they hesitant on spending for a great hockey player, especially if he or she can play outside & inside hockey nor do they hesitate on getting best care for their players.

The game has been started the referees and players are in place the NHL puck has been dropped. The control opens up with the Penguins, a left shot quick center quick right and the pack ends up behind the goal. The Detroit Red Wings take control of the puck. The choose to go straight down center; then a sharp right-back center-their quick response to the puck yields them 1 point shoaling under goalies legs. 1-0 Detroit longing the puck into play dropping the puck Detroit side near center of goalie. The Penguins regain control. Their pace or play is slower taking time to set up a shot striking the puck 12 times before an attempt for a point. Detroit's goalie is on top on blacks the shot, but not before a foul by Penguins. As the game progresses the score has advanced 3 Penguins 2 Red Wings Red Wings control puck. Their quickness to get the puck in line for a goal pays off as it only takes 3 shots on the left & one shot down center goal. The last quarter buzzer sounds a 5 min break to get refreshed by both teams is in order. The game resumes with the puckey dropped at center court. Possession Red Wings. With their quickness down quart on Penguin slips between two Red Wing players and steels the puck. The Penguins control the puck 3½ minutes & 3¼ minutes they score their 4th goal giving them the lead 3-4-1¼ minutes ¾ minutes the Red Wings in position to tie ¼ min shot Detroit time out their last ½ minuet remains, Detroit looks at the line up of Pittsburg two choices either quickly center or 3 quick left shots. They puck 3 left shots hoping the 3rd shot throws of Penguins defense: a Penguin again steels the puck before the third shot.

The Penguins pass the puck carefully and slowly running time out. The clock is the Penguins friend. Once again the Penguins show their slowness is time well spent.

Note: Conclusion

The Penguins slowness shows once again time spent on development of a play is Time Well Spent

The Athlete

DONALD KEITH LIKED SPORTS. IN high school Dunbar Elementary and in college. He always entered into a sports program; called the Athlete Curriculum. The program not only a one sport program. Donald's Program was designed for a variety of sports. You pick; then we will train; you for 4 sports. Donald liked it. We chose all four of the top programs.

Donald worked hard training in all four of his best liked sports.

Amazing none was baseball basketball football or even racket ball. None sports programs he chose had any kind of ball.

Swimming was his favorite sport. His best swimming trait was the butterfly event once he mastered it, he swam in a number of swimming events and all-way the butterfly event. That was his best swim. Swimming was not the only thing he was good at. Donald was good in track, his best time for a mile event was 7.02 hours. Every evening Donald practice his running. He would run around the school's track in 4.09 min. Only one other could run faster Bill Gates had the school record of 2.89 minutes. Donald had two more years of high school left his goal before leaving was to become the best runner in the track event before he graduated. For this week his goal was 3.97½ minutes that would put him second best fastest no one else was even close.

Donald third chosen event was ball free also. It was badminton; even though the birdie was shopped like a ball on the front end it was not considered a ball event. Donald 6 teammates rotated positions making each a master at all positions, like the other events Donald put his best effort forward.

Donald had yet another sports event he liked roller skating.

Again Donald did his best and would settled for nothing less. Again it was a team effort, Donald was faster, stronger, and more skilled than the rest. He had been roller skating since 6 years of age, he watched it on T.V. and studied every aspect on T.V. He also added a couple of his skills. He even used skills of those who taught him about roller skating; and roller derbies altogether Donald was at pro level on all four events. Accomplishment few other had. Even in the pro ranks.

Donald never finished lower than third and seldom did he not give it his best shot.

After 8 years of competing in all four of his best liked events Donald no longer was contender with lower than pro statise. At the beginning of his 9th year Donald was named The Athlete of the Year his 10th year Donald; he was named The All Around Athlete having more trophies in all four of his competitive events.

He had won the best honors than any athlete total and in every event

Donald was retired as the only athlete to have won first place trophies is 4 athletic events. As time passed Donald was called The Athlete.

The Bird's Nest

SHERWIN WAS FLYING HOME WHEN he saw rain clouds ahead. He decided to go another route home. There were dangers though. It was threw a heavily thick forest.

Flying threw was tricky. He had to duck threw branches that had hardly any clearance.

Also a lot of trees grew over 20 foot high. Flying 28 foot was his top flight. Sherwin had the roteriteal of flying higher; but he did not want to risk it.

This time he did stretch it. He flew 33¼ feet in the air. Well above most trees in the forest. High enough to see Loni's Nest. He could see her minding her nest with twigs from the ground. Sherwin decided to land by Loni she was fetching twigs from the ground when Sherwin landed inches from her. She jumped aside startled by Sherman's sudden appearance.

Sherwin grabbed some twigs laying on the ground. He offered them to Loni. She hesitated for a moment then accepted them. Heck it saved her from carrying them he was great help. She no longer had to fly down to the ground and back up with a beak full of twigs or straw either.

Loni got use to Sherwin. Together they built a larger nest than Loni had planned on. Loni liked the larger nest she could flap her wings further out. The perch was larger also extending 2¼" from the nest. Giving Loni a running distance before she leaped into the sky for a much better flight.

Sherwin pulled the twigs as tight as he could. Giving the nest a stronger body.

Loni thanked Sherwin for his help. "No problem," Sherwin replied.

Loni tidied up. Sherwin left Loni's nest and flew back to his. It was 3 years ago when Sherwin made his birds nest. It was starting to come apart. Sherwin had made small repairs. The major repair work Sherwin planned on making repairs; but never got wound to it. The major destruction was beyond repair. Looks like Sherwin will need to make another birds nest.

Sherwin flew around looking for porch & walnut. They were strong woods. The bark from both would

Sherwin still was making repairs to Loni's nest. It had been damaged by a wind storm.

Loni would stay @ Sherwin's nest when Sherwin did major repair work.

Sherwin was glad to have Loni share his home. Him sharing his nest would create a bond between them.

Full filled with his repair Sherwin was also getting fulfilled with Loni sharing his home. They were becoming more friendly and were getting closer. Their friendship lead to Loni becoming a full time resident at Sherwin's and that lead to a relationship that would be them living in one birds nest like husband & wife.

Bully and the Wolfe

O**N THE SOUTHERN PORTS SHIP** sail into the docks some are only docked an hour or so. Some dock for weeks at a time or months hardly ever does a boat of any size dock a whole year.

Bully James retired from ship's captain of the cruise liner he had took 40 years ago. Things have changed longer trips, food menu that was served on the ship changed. Name of the places he had sailed to where the ships travel log.

Bully applied for captain of other ships but they told him to retire. Retire "NO" said Bully I have a lot of experience that should land me a job on another cruise liner. Bully applied at boat travel locations all over. No one wanted a 72 year old ship captain even if he did sail to a lot of places around the world.

Bully decided he would take his friends advice and re-tire from being a cruise liner captain. Bull packed up his ocean and sea gear. He rented a storage bend by the year. Maybe someday he would find another captains job.

Bully pack up a backpack full of clothing and cooling & camping gear; bought a pair of hiking boots some genes bought a hunting knife and headed away from the sailing docks.

An old dirt road partially filled with chips of stone, (where it once was a stone road).

Bully followed the old road that once was made of stone. He followed it until there no more was a road.

Now a path Bully thought to follow the path; after all it once was a part of the stone road system.

Bully followed the path into the mountains. It was a lot of climbing. Bully was use to flat lands hardly did he ever climb to get around a mountain. He just went around it at it's base where the land was flat.

But even hiking had changed mostly people climbed mountains. Bully bought some rope and steel daw that would dig into the mountains, so he could pull himself up the mountain.

Bully had one been hiking around the mountain side 3 months. He was classifying himself as a junior climber. He had a lot more to learn about climbing; especially when he was faced with high rugged mountains.

Bully camped on a ledge midway up the mountain he was climbing. He built a fire; it was cold midway up the mountain.

Bully was almost asleep when he heard a noise it sounded like metal scraping on rock. Bully went to check it out.

The noise came closer slowly it approached Bully finally it came into the light.

A wolf with a collar that had a chain attached. Someone had chained the wolf up. Bully patted his arm and clapped his hands. Then waved his arms towards his chest. The wolf with chain made its way to Bully.

Bully wrestled with the chain until it was free from the collar. Bully patted the wolf and gave it some other chowder.

Bully went to sleep with the wolf at his feet. At first sun up the wolf howled. It wake Bully. Bully wanted to sleep longer but since he was awake he wake the wolf. Bully tried to push the wolf away from him but it kept coming back to his hind legs. Bully threw packs at the wolf but it dodged them and kept following him. Bully went into a "cafe" but the wolf hung around outside waiting for Bully to come out.

Bully figured he had a friend in the wolf. But Bully did not want a pet they are just like a woman. They need commitment; or any family.

Bully quit feeding the wolf but the wolf caught its own food rabbits, gophers; field mice it even ate fruit and vegetables from the fruit trees that grew wild and from gardens that had been abandon.

Bully went home from his day out visiting his friends when he got home the wolf was there waiting for Bully to return home. Bully reached out and petted the wolf. Old buddy guess I'm stuck with you. Bully let the wolf into his cabin Bully made it a bed by the log burning stove. Bully taught the wolf to catch fish specifically blue gill. But other kind would do when hungry. Bully taught the wolf to fetch a ball and in the evening Bully and the wolf played together. Bully thought of a name for the wolf. He called it Buddy.

The Silver Dollar

JAY AND LETHA OWNED A restaurant in Peorea Illinois. It is rated a four star restaurant. To live up to its four star rating Jay and Letha needed to give it a name worthy of its four star rating.

Jay suggested Jay & Letha's; Letha said no. Jay also suggested Mom's Restaurant. Still they did not agree on a name. Letha came up with some of her own suggestions for a name for the restaurant; one was The Last Restaurant, because it was setting away from any town. Another name she thought of was Caffine Café because they served a lot of coffee.

The day of the opening of the restaurant neither Jay nor Letha had thought of a name for their restaurant.

Since they could not agree on a name why not led the clients of the restaurant name? "How about" Letting them name it through a suggestion box or by Jay and Letha agreed on having a raffle. The winner or winners would be naming the restaurant.

Jay went to a ticket sales booth. He bought 1,000.

Jay returned to Letha's home together they came up with a plan to name the restaurant. Letha had several boxes of envelopes. Both of them set at a table and began putting raffle tickets in them the mailing them everywhere. It was 3 week until they received their first returned address with names to name their restaurant. Letter came back from 70% of the letters mailed out.

Jay put at the mails in his tray-Letha took in all email suggestions, some of the mail names were Burt's. Some were the Lone Coffee. That one might be considered female names were Hellens; The Last Female Restaurant.

Jay and Silver Coffee. She liked the silver part of the name. She choose it as her part of the restraints name. Jay would choose the last part.

That would be even harder; even though Letha had already chosen the first name of the restaurant Jay was walking down the street. He hardly knew it was raining he was pacing up & down trying to choose his part of the restaurant name. It began to rain Jay pulled his hat over his head to keep his eyes clear. As he walk he passed throw a puddle a glimpse of something shinny.

The Allwells

MR. ALLWELL AN INSURANCE SALES rep; one afternoon was going some house to house in a new neighborhood that his company had as new client prospects.

Mr. Allwell Monroe Insurance agency. Mr. Allwell Ronnie he was called by his first name at the agency.

Ronnie was given a list of 15 names that was transferring their insurance to Monroe. The first person on the list was Mr Garber he had accidental insurance and was changing to full coverage.

Ronnie spent just 15 min with Mr. Garber and he was signed as a Monroe policy. The second person on the list was Mr. & Mrs. Terell. They had separate policies they wanted to combine them into one policy that insured both. The third person Miss Connie West. Mr. Allwell not only sold her a full coverage policy. He sold her himself. It was a romance made for the both of them. They went on a date that very evening. Then another a week later, it became a continues dating affair, for the next 10 months of the year. After the 10 month it became an affair little dating a connection between them for the rest of their life. They spent every hour they could together. It went on for 2 years.

Ronnie and Miss Connie, he called her by her last name. He said "We've been dating and a close affair with one another how about we get married?" Miss Connie's eyes widened her hazel eyes twinkled more than they had ever. Her heart rate rose and she began to breathe deeply.

Oh would I ever she said then grabbed him by the head and kissed him, they set the date for Thanksgiving at 5:00 pm. It was a Tuesday. Right away Connie had invitations made and ordered food from a banquet. The honeymoon was in no other than Niagra Falls. 2 weeks at the falls in the luxury motel across from the falls.

Two years later, Connie was birthing her first child a boy they named Ronnie Jounier. Born on the 4th of July. Their second also a boy they named Eddie Wayne Allwell. It was 3 years latter a third boy they named Danny. Their total married life the birthed 7 children, all boys.

A large family indeed and all still living together.

Connie & Ronnie are now 42 years old still a lot of living kids. Of course Ronnie Jounier is the eldest of the 7 boys. James the youngest. I won't name all seven or tell their stories it would take too pages. A lot of writing.

Ronnie began to think he had 7 boys all strong after conversing with all seven then agreed to become farmers. Pooling their monies together they came up with enough money to buy 50 acres of farm land. Ronnie would keep his job @ Monroes Insurance for farm money, supplies, seed, plows, tractor, shovels or anything they would need for farm equipment.

Ronnie had 3 clients for his insurance. They were spread throughout the day. He left the boys with the farm chores assigning each one a specific job. Then work together with remaining farm chores that included house. And one of the boys I did not name was to water the plants. No matter what kind it was. Harvest was coming next week, start of picking season. Luckily, they owned a picker, a machine that picks 100 or more at once.

Mr. Allwell clients for his farm is grocery stores in valley. Also he makes deliveries to restaurants and banquets. Sometimes he just set out in front of his home with crates full of vegetables. 100.00 A bushel or after business day free vegetables so they will not spoil.

Coming up to the farm house people are invited in for a free meal of vegetables. Soups mostly as salads or from the east side where the sun shines in fruit is grown and fruit salads are made. Sold for 50¢ during business day. After business day; give the vegetables free fruit baskets salads or just plain fruit like apples and peaches.

While everyone was enjoying the fruits and veggies the Allwells prepared for the next days business. After that they were pleased to see everyone was indeed having a good time.

Buck Eye Strong
Woody Payne

Woody Payne could do no harm, she was quite a gall.
Woody was 5'4 inch tall. Hazel eyes; coal black hair; shoulder length. Breast size 38 x 33.

Woody learned the skills of a singer. Her voice was that of a soprano. Her choice of singing style was that of her church. She was a member of Saint Hellan Christian Church. She was a quire singer. She stood on the outside of row three. Mary was an important part of the quire, most of the songs sang required a soprano.

Not only did Mary sing for the church quire; she went out to the community and helped Pastor Robert. She also helped cook at church outings. She cooked pot pies; potatoes; collie flower; casseroles; pies; cherry apple, and peach.

When she was not doing things for the church she was doing them for the community.

Mary gave little time for herself. What little time she did use for herself was doing jobs of the house hold, laundry; dishes; cleaning, clothing, rooms in the house, windows and furniture in the house.

When Mary wake from her slumber (sleep) the first thing she did was clean her eyes out, then clean her whole body. Once she cleaned herself she rubbed herself down with a body cream.

Once Mary thought she was thoroughly clean, she went to the church to clean, she was cleaning 16 hours a day. The only reason she was not cleansing was she was in transit to next cleaning area or preparing the tools she used to clean with. She also never cleaned during services of the church. It is said Father Robert's has the cleanest church in the valley.

Wood did though squeeze in 4 hours 20 hours a week for herself. Woody still made time for entertainment activities. She doing @ church socials outside his church, she also sang at private church organizations.

Woody had used up all her wake time, she had some business coming in; it would have to be done from her slumber time. There would be 3 new business. She would be working with Donnie and Marries Sanctuary, a burial firm called peace of mind burials. The third was a banquet company that serviced marriages, family & private.

Woody liked listening to other people sing once a week she looked in the newspaper in the entertainment section. She looked for musical & comedy entertainment. She preferred it to be of a God nature or church tune. Just two days ago there was a priest telling what people asked him about was if holiday came day before church and he went to church before did the he need to go the regular church day.

Father Roberts also was asked sports concerning prayer-church. If you shot a ball in golf 140 yard on a golf course do you need to pray to thank god for the ball going as far as it went or pray before you swing your club? If you shoot a basketball from above the key. Pray that it goes through the hoop. If you kick a field goal pray before you kick it or after it goes through the upright!

Father Robert's answer was both times and during flight.

Woody still sings for the church. She also now records music under her name it is called Woody Paynes Top Religious songs. Some is gospel, some is from hymn book at church she learned; some from the cathedrals she had been in and somewhere not even church music originally. They were Hillbilly songs country songs and blue grass; songs that she incorporated into her music as church songs. All together her CD's now but started as recordings then records tapes.

Woody spends her time now writing songs, and others that maybe thought of as having religious words in them.

Robbie and the Butterflies

Robbie Lang lived in a cottage all by himself. He had white and yellow curtains an all 6 windows. 2 windows to a side his back and front yards had lilly pads in the ponds that was in the back and front yards. A dirt drive way ran from the right side of the cottage and 4 foot from the right side, of the house. His grass was a dark green.

Robbie kept up his yard; not only Robbie had the kind of flower's that attracts butterflies.

Every spring a herd of butterflies swarmed his flowers.

Robbie did not shoo the butterflies away, he knew they pollinized them. Robbie lifed seeing the butterflies and their many different colors. But flowers were not their food source. Their food source was the fallen once it was spread all over a flower. They also like the stems of the flowers.

Robbie thought since there were so many butterflies he would build a home for some of them.

Robbie went to the lumber yard and bought some wood nails and glue enough to build 15 butterfly houses.

Robbie gathered all the wood. He took it home and started making the butterfly homes. Ten of them planted all around the yard. To attract butterflies, Robbie put flower peddles and fish oil in every butterfly home.

Not soon after butterflies came in packs. They flew from one butterfly home to the other and they spread there. As the years passed more & more butterflies came.

Robbie walked among the butterflies; as he walked they landed on him. It was like he was giving them a free ride around his yard. From one flower to the other.

Robbie liked it when the butterflies landed on his shoulder and his short. When he got tired of them he shook his shoulder and they would fly away.

Sometimes Robbie played with them running around shaking them off his body then letting them land on him again.

There were no favorite butterflies it was a little hard distinguishing one from the other whenever Robbie played with the butterflies. It was not just a couple at a time but a multiple (a bunch) at a time.

Robbie put food out 5 times a day butterflies eat a lot.

When Robbie was not playing with them he was playing with his pet dog Ruffous.

Robbie also had a friend he would play with Jarried. Robbie spent more time with the butterflies than he did Ruffous; or any of his friends.

Robbie enjoyed his friends the butterflies, Robbies butterflies everyone called them; and the began to call Robbie The Butterfly Man.

There wasn't a time you did not see Robbie without a butterfly somewhere on his body.

Robbie missed them when they flew down south. They went there every year to mate. That was another reason Robbie could not give any one butterfly a name. They were so much alike you could not tell which butterfly was. The only way Robbie could tell a specific butterfly from another was if its wing was tore in a certain area.

There were so many butterflies on Robbies land that they covered his backyard where he had planted many flowers. Chasing them away was not an option. They only returned before he could get back into the house.

T

Mee-Mo

JAMES MEAN LIVES ON A house boat. He is the captain; owner of a 7'4" houseboat. There is two deck the lower deck has 6 rooms on each side. A floor between the left rooms and right rooms. At the front is the captains sleeping room in the back is a mens & a womans restroom. The top deck in the far side (back) is nothing again from the back to the front a flat wooden floor.

In the front the steering wheel a wooden compass next to the steering wheel far front a map room with 2 beds (twin)-one captains the other his assistant.

The house boat is an old ship converted to a house boat.

James has loved the sea ever since he was 8 years of age. He and his parents sailed on a house boat to upper New York then on to New Hampshire where they settled.

When James was 12 he and his father built a small paddle boat. They went fishing in it. James since then has bought his own houseboat. He tied paddle boats to the sides; 4 in all.

He sails up and down the Atlantic Ocean. He made his house boat a tour boat $10.00 25 miles. 10 miles from shore. Sometimes James unties one of the paddle boats grabs a pole made of lime; two a non string to the pole plus a head no 7 hook, a strong hook; he fishes for polk and swordfish.

On evening just before night fall; James was fishing when an 8-feet shark jumped out of the water; almost knocking him out of the boat.

James grabbed the ors and paddled as fast as he could towards the houseboat.

The large shark followed James jumping in and out of the water. James sped up his paddling. He made it to the house boat hooked it up to a pull and pulled himself up the side of the houseboat.

James thought that would be the last of the shark. Not true. It had jumped a board-James approached the 8 foot fish. It had broken a fin. It was chasing James to get its fin repaired.

James did just that with a thin rope and a large hook James sowed the fishes fin back on. He gave it a big pat on the top of its head. Then threw it back into the sea.

That was not the last of the 8 footer James would see it.

When James went to sea with his houseboat the fish would great James back.

James realized the giant of fishes would great James and his houseboat whenever they came to sea.

James decided to give him a name. No need tagging him you could see a 4 inch wide 2 foot long light white streak where its fin was.

James took first 3 letters from his name; dropping the n. Then he paused (a high phen). Mo from Mom dropped the last m. "Mee-Mo" That is what I'll call you. The large shark learned his name quickly.

When James was at sea and spotted Mee-Mo, he called out Mee Mo as loud as he could. Mee Mo came. Mee-Mo streaked through the water jumping as he went. Mee-Mo was at the side of the house boat. When he saw James he jumped aboard.

James had made a water trough on the right side of the boat. Mee Mo jumped in, so did James. The played together, they both were happy they were back together.

After a half hour together Mee-Mo jumped out of the trough and back into the sea. A half hour was the longest he could stay out of the sea. The trough was not deep enough and Mee Mo need to get back so he could chase down a couple mouth fulls of fish. When in the sea Mee Mo chased fish all day long.

Fish was not all Mee Mo ate. He also ate a lot of sea moss and sea turtles.

James turned the house boat upstream to pick up some passengers. They had reserved the houseboat for a wedding.

James hired a food service to set up a banquet luncheon of meet. The banquet began and James' steered the house boat down stream.

Mee-Mo did not know there was a banquet in the houseboat he splashed up from the sea and landed near his water trough. Water splashed all over the floor near the trough. It also splashed on some of the passengers. They began to run to the other side.

James went to Mee-Mo. He gave him a pat on the head, then rushed him back into the sea. Mee Mo was shocked and thought James did not like him anymore. Mee-Mo never returned to the house boat, James searched but soon gave up. The never saw each other again.

Sherod The River of The Sherwin People

SHEROD BEGAN HIGH ON A mountain called The Mountain of the Silver Back Caverns.

The Sherod began its journey out of a cavern called Silver Cavern. Called that because it took on the coloration of silver coloration of the valley.

Sherod flowed over silver colored rock and pebbles. Making its way down ward to the valley below then out into a sea of silver that had turned from a sky blue to the coloration of the silver that had flowed into at its beaches.

From its north banks to its southern banks the once sky blue sea had turned not from a light silver but to a dark midnight silver.

The Sherwin people of the Elders faintly remembered the sky blue coloration of the sea they called the sea Silver.

They described it as uncluttered sea that lay still and untouched. A sea of purity that provided a clear water free of debry for the many people came to the sky blue sea to drink and collect the water to take back to their own homes to drink and cook with.

They came with vails & buckets, they carried long leather pouches; empty. They filled them money. Using wild feathered four legged moose. The cold weather of the lands made it impossible for any others animal or otherwise to travel into a valley that was shinny and had pure water in its sea.

As the years passed the moose had adapted to the unfeeling and harsh weather of the silver mountains. The now feathered moose had not only grown feathers to keep off the chill of the freezing weather, it also grew stronger; giving it strength to carry many vails and leather pouches of water.

Once at the sea of sky blue color the Sherwin people filled their containers with the sky blue water.

After a couple days of rest the Sherwin people began their journey home.

A journey much harder than their journey to the sea of blue. A journey unlike the path they had fallen to the sky blue sea, but a path through much harder had to be moved. To remove these walls, it took many hours of labor hard sweating and straining labor.

The Sherwin people were rough muscular people from their young lives to their elderly lives. They made their way lack to their homes with 82% of the sky blue water they had packed up in their vails and leather water bags.

Dean and Samson

DEAN WENT TO THE LIVING room window. She was checking out the weather.

It was raining; she could see the raindrops bursting when they splashed up against the window; then running down toward the window sash.

With a frown on her face Dean turned around and went back to the couch. She pulled her legs up to the cushion. Then crossed her legs.

She was waiting on Samson but he had told her if it rained he would not leave until the rain stopped.

Dean grabbed a book from the end table on the right of the couch. The table was a glass table. The book was called Bear Tracks. Dean was on the second chapter. She put on her glasses; they were a third grade. She could not read without them.

The book was about a bear hunter named Samson, Dean turned the page. The book read The black bear ran into the woods; Samson the Bear Hunter ran after the black bear. Dean turned the page. Samson had lost the bear.

Dean like the courage of Samson, he had the nerve of Davey Crockett a historic bear tracker.

Samson followed the bear track that lead into the woods.

Dean turned the page. She read on while chasing the black bear. Samson ran into some white bears.

Samson backed away and watched them. It was the first time Samson had encountered a white bear.

Samson hid behind a red wood tree. He had no idea that the white bear would do?

Would it attack or just walk on buy or stand to protect its 2 cubs it had with it?

Samson took no chances. He let the white bear and her cubs pass. He did not want to hurt the mom & her cubs. If he killed the mother bear the cubs would be orphans.

The black bear tracks had crossed the white bear tracks. Samson found them once the white bear tracks were behind him.

Dean was so far into the book she had to finish it; two chapters left.

Dean turned the page to chapter 8. The heading read The Black Bear Meets A Female Bear.

Samson made camp he lit the two campfires to keep any wild animals away not just bears. Samson slept light he knew there was bears around both black and white.

Dean read on to the next chapter.

Samson and the Wolf was the 9th chapter. Samson woke to the sound of a wolfs howl. It was a red wolf. Red wolfs liked eating bears; black or white or brown. The wolf did not care if the bear was red black white or brown. He liked the fight of taking down the large animal.

Samson was fearful of the wolf. If he could take down a large bear what would it do to him?

Dean turned to the last page of chapter 9. The last chapter, 10th chapter titled Samson Meets Antelope.

Dean could not wait to see how Samson handled the antelope. The antelope was fast with its 5 foot high legs. It stroke its prey quickly. Samson was use to either slow animals or medium strength of running power.

Samson looked for a safe place. Dean read on. Samson had idea about the antelope it was fast, it stroke fast, it also could carry heavy loads. Samson needed any to travel. He made a saddle of cloth and wood. For three month Samson trained the antelope to carry him and his hunting gear. The book ends with Samson Traveling Around With His Trained Antelope.

Dean closed the book. She liked it better than any book she had read.

The Flower That Grew Too Tall

Johny not the name of a man, but a young girl who liked to flowers. Johny planted flowers every spring and all the way tell the last day of spring.

Starting with a single seed from a magnolia. Johny planted it in a milk cartoon, full of dirt. Every day after planting the seed Johny watered it and put flower dust from another magnolia. They all grew to their normal size. So did the other magnolias that sprang up from the original magnolia that grew out of the milk box. There was no need for Johny to identify the magnolia that grew so tall it bent over the milk box. The rest were of normal size when it was being talked about everyone called it the Grant Magnolia. Johny thought it was strange that the magnolia grew as high as it did. Johny decided she would cut the stem below the magnolia then replant the magnolia. After the replanting the magnolia started its regrowth. Once again the magnolia grew tall. It grew to be larger than before. Johny could not believe the height that the magnolia was growing. The magnolia not only grew higher but its offspring multiplied but none grew to a height the original magnolia grew.

Johny went to the flower garden. She walked over to the roses; she had every color red rose; white; rose; blue and yellow roses. Her favorite was the lavender roses. She liked the smell of them. She also liked the color of lavender.

Samson thought a rose is a rose and a dandelion is a dandelion.

Johny liked planting flowers in a maze formation. She also liked planting them in rows. Johny had a flower everywhere she had room to plant them. So no one would step on them and shake their peddles off.

Johny would not mind if a person picked one and plucked the peddles off. What she did not like was them walking over or near enough to disturb the peddles. Their was an area nearby that had no flowers at all. Johny roped it off; dug a three inch deep 24 inch wide trench. The first 6 inches she planted orange tulips. The next six inches blue tulips. Then a six inch row of daffodils.

For the next 6 inches marigolds. Then crocuses. Only 12 inches of land left to plant on.

It was in her third year of her flower garden that she began to sell the flowers she grew.

After talking to others on what their prices were she decided to split the difference. All flowers were the same price a flower on a stem 25 cents seeds 40 cents a package.

Johny had bought 10 dozen small bags. She put 12 seeds in each.

Johny was proud of her garden. She had the best flower garden around people could not say a thing bad about Johnnies flower garden.

Johnies garden got so big acreage wise that she had to hire gardeners to help with the maintenence of them. The gardeners arrived at 2:01 P.M. First they checked for insects; if they found insects they sprayed them with alcohol. They next checked the dirt at the bottom of the flower that went into the ground. They were checking for sturdiness. After caring for a single flower and there were 1245 full grown Johnny liked her flower garden and the spent the rest of her life bettering it.

The House That Stands Alone

FAR FROM JERSEY TURNPIKE A row mountain tops shows its peaks and it's frozen snow to the volley below.

At the bottom base spread out on the lands pine and spruce trees exhibits a variety of leaf shapes and colors. Green grass with white lilies and yellow tulips.

Puddles from recent snowfall from the Jersey Mountain widens each and every puddle.

Set in the middle of the bottom land is a lone house. One story high with a brick smoke stack that has a grayish with smoke drifting into the air far above the white snow peaks of the mountains.

The smoke stack comes from a wood burning fire place inside the house at the middle of the only room.

The room has wooden floor and thin plywood walls. The walls covered with wall paper with an army of soldiers coming out of the mountains caverns.

A pug laying on the floor un-stabilized; embroided from a round spool of brown three inch thick twine.

Setting on the 30 x 30 Dghare rug is a black potbelly stove.

From the stove, dark white smoke with the smell of pine. The pine smell was from branches from the pine trees outside on top of the stove. Two kettles made of cast iron; sent more hazy smoke into the air; that drifted to the fire place and mixed with the smoke going into the smoke stack through the whole length and out into the outside air.

The house stands alone no people in it, no animals that was astray had entered it. Nor any fowl made its way inside the house.

The house appeared empty but for the pot belly stove and the two iron kettles atop the stove.

How could it be? Someone had to light the fire in the pot belly stove.

Debbie was the house keeper of the house that stood alone. Early in the morning around 4 AM Debbie opened the front door to the house that stood alone.

She would first light the stove from the logs she had put in it the night before. Debbie filled the trio from pots with cold water. One for coffee & tea and one for soup. They were all in a box on a small table beside pot belly stove.

Once the pots were hat she set them on the edge to keep them hot for the coffee; tea; and soups.

Debbie returned the next evening. She refilled both pots and re-supplied the coffee; tea; and soups.

It was odd that in a house that stood in a valley all alone was always well supplied with coffee tea & soup.

It was also odd that the smoke came out of the chimney in an empty house.

Everyone knew Debbie was the care taker of the house that stood alone. If anything they were sospishas that there was no water in the pots or coffee, tea or soups was not setting on a small table beside the pot belly stove.

They also thought it to be odd if it was always empty. (The House)

But then who was to check if not Debbie. If Debbie did not fill the pots and put wood in the fire and set fire to it, for the coffee tea or soups who did?

"No one!" because Debby was the keeper of the house that stood alone. And only her. How did Debbie accomplish her daily choirs without missing a single time?

She had a room to her own built on the house that stood alone. It only appeared to be empty. Debbie was always there.

My Dog Ajax

Walking home one day. I Rodger Jenning came across a pet shop.

It was full of all types of animals–parrots; fish; dogs and cats, and other types of animals. I saw an iguana that kind of took to my liking.

It had large blue eyes a large long tail and tiny paws.

Another creature took to my liking a middle sized Sheppard. It was a light brown with a furry tail, eyes of golden yellow. It was a cheerful little fellow and very playful.

My decision on what kind of pet I was to buy came from my attraction.

The pet store employee Mr. Perry gave me a discount $20.00 off if I bought the furry little Sheppard? I looked around at the others that I was attracted to, but when the Sheppard shook his long tail raised his paw to me; then licked me on my arm, I knew this little Sheppard with the golden eyes; long tail and outreached paw; was the animal of my choosing.

The total cost a small charge of $35.00.

I was shy about 3.75. Okay $31.75. I reached in my billfold I had $31.00 in paper money and one penny less than 75 cents. I gave my pockets a search for the remaining penny. None there. I am in desperate search for the remaining penny, I reached down to my folded up jeans; a small cuff. Going from front to back on right leg nothing but dirt; rocks and sand, I undid the cuff and emptied it. I searched the other leg produced the remaining penny.

I handed it to the pet store employee. In return he snapped on a leather leach on a neck collar. Then handed me the end of the leach. I had no problem at all the Sheppard gladly followed me out of the pet store. The little Sheppard hurriedly moved his legs & paws to keep up with my slow walking pace.

When we reached my home as soon as I went inside my front door, I removed the leech from the little fellow's collar. He jumped up into my arms. I barely caught him. I let the little guy roam the house; so he could get use to the whole house. I had stopped at a store before I went to the pet shop and bought a book on animal names.

It was listed alphabetically; in types of animals. Again alphabetically in name. I had gone down the list of dog names gender female first I skipped to male starting with the A names I had only gotten to AJ. When I came to the name Ajax. After saying Ajax to the Sheppard four or five times he began to bark in a squeaky high pitched bark. From then on he when I called out Ajax he barked and came running as fast as his little legs & paws could move.

Now that we had established his name I began to teach Ajax a couple tricks. I had bought a couple dog toys. A ball red; white and blue was one I rolled it across my living room floor. The first couple times Ajax just stood and watched it roll to a stop. I took about 20 rolls before he started chasing the red white and blue ball.

I guess my next trick was set. I took twice as long to teach Ajax to set as it did to teach him to chase the red white and blue ball.

After a month Ajax had learned 10 tricks. By the end of the year Ajax had a trick total of 35 tricks. Ajax had grown a little in a year almost twice the size when I bought him.

Ajax and I became lifelong buddies.

Ruby Rockwell

R UBY ROCKWELL WAS A STRAIGHT A student, but Ruby had no interest in the school social activities.

Ruby separated herself from her school after graduation. A year later, Ruby enrolled in University of Colorado. Although Ruby was from West Virginia Ruby left her home state. Ruby had seen films of Colorado University and its surroundings. It was not the university that attracted Ruby to Colorado. It was Colorado's beautiful landscape around the university. The tall cactus with white flowers. Ruby entered Colorado University as a Nature Major with a science minor Ruby was not so much interested in science as she was in Nature.

She was not only interested in the plant life that grew in Colorado, she was also a fan of Colorado wild animal life.

The animals that were natural.

Ruby had a high intelligence about the natural side of Colorado.

Ruby received her bachelor's degree in Nature. She was hired by a firm called The Colorado State Parks Company.

Ruby's worked as a Park Scientist. After a year's study of 4 parks, Ruby had come up with some interesting facts about each of the 4-parks she had been working in.

Ruby had discovered that the insect life survival was a system of relying on other creatures that was small. They kind of worked like a company not one thing worked on its own a network of other components made somewhere specific then going down a conveyor belt sometimes different parts of a conveyor belt that is going off in another direction. A track that took to a final direction where like parts were stored or to a place where parts were assembled to make a whole part final product.

Ruby and 40 other Nature explorers went to the Green Forrest, called that because of the abundant green plant life and trees full of a dark green color.

Ruby and her friend were not looking for anything in-specific. They came across some green beetles; making their nest in a hollowed out maple tree green leafs with a yellow flower.

Ruby and Cleo (Rubies friend) studied the beetles watching their daily routine; as they traveled to their nest from an apple tree near buy then from their nest to the apple tree.

The next day they studied deer watching them as they searched for food for their young. The deer used a sneak attack to capture their prey.

Their third day it was the white bear. The following day elk; then buffalo

They not only studied the life of plants and trees. Ruby and Cleo both earned their masters and both become forest rangers in two different places. Ruby and Cleo kept in touch writing one another about the exciting creatures that lived in each of their forest.

They found that some were related to an animal or insect and even plants were related to some kind in each forest.

Ruby and Cleo started a nature club in both forest. The traveled both forest studying creatures and plant life of both forest.

It was 10 years later when both forest grew together and became one.

Ruby and Cleo remained friends for life and became partners in the nature exploration of both now one forest. That took the name of the green forest.

The Flower Gardens

MARTHA HILLMAN LIVED NEAR THE Hillshire Flower Gardens. People from all around visited the gardens from April to September in the north. In the south were a lot more flower sanitariums and gardens that's what made the southern states.

Martha had heard about the flowers of Italy and France. The whole world talked about the beautiful flowers in Europe. The flowers became an invite to the tropics with their inter twinning and eventually all by their selves cross breading that widened their notoriety.

Martha's love of flowers intrigued her to make Flower Genealogy her major in college, for her minor was the rain forest.

After receiving a bachelors in both Flower Genealogy and the Rain Forrest, she ventured out to the rain forest with a large assortment of flowers.

As the years passed more and more flower genetics were developed by the cross breading of flowers.

Flowers with hard to pronounce names spread across the earth. Some glowing in area's that used to be a dessert were nothing grew.

Martha left the rain forest and the new genetic of flowers.

She returned to her home where she had already had a flower. Martha spent her life growing and sometimes inventing flowers. Her gardens grew to 50 acers. That's where she drew the line.

If there was a flower she had not herd of she would pay to the person who had such a flower; and add it gladly to her 50 acres of flowers. Their hallway was room for newly invented flower.

Jerry Giraffe

WHILE WORKING OUT THE MANAGER had Mike call him Jerry. The East Missouri Zoo; called the Missouri Animal Kingdom had many new orphan animals, a new barn giraffe stumbled around from one side of his habitat to the other a year old and twice as tall as the older giraffes. Still had no name. Everyone at the zoo agreed; it was time to give the large giraffe a name. The came up with several names Cidd was one. That was too common. Harry was another to easy it also was a very common name. 89 was a third name no one agreed on.

After trying out 50 names that did not suit the large giraffe. The manager Jerry was a tall dude. 5 inch taller than anyone at the zoo. Jerry was able to see farther than anyone else; because he was taller.

The giraffe no had yet been named could also see a lot further than anyone or animal at the zoo. That included the manager Jerry after deliberating for a couple hours. The zoo employees agreed on a name. The only one that came up more than any name. It was the manager of the zoo's name. Jerry. It seemed natural because Jerry and the giraffe could see the furthest.

For the next 2 month everyone called the giraffe Jerry. Finally one day the giraffe responded to its name Jerry. When someone called out Jerry the giraffe new it he they were calling out to.

Jerry the manager had to be called Jerry Zoo keeper; so every one new who they were speaking of. That was okay with Jerry. He was flattered the zoo employees named the giraffe after him.

From the day everyone called out for Jerry Giraffe; Jerry the Zoo Keeper waited to see who was calling out Jerry's name. When he figured out which one they were talking to, Jerry the Zoo keeper/manager either answered or went on about his business at the zoo.

When Jerry the Giraffe herd the name he came winning up to the person call out his name. When he approached the person he licked them with his huge tongue. Jerry's lick in the face showed them he was friendly and he liked them.

Sometimes Jerry would let children ride him like a horse. Adults wanted to control him; he did not like that. When a child rode him he could take his time or gallop like a horse would besides it was more fun when children rode him.

Jerry's long legs enabled him to go further in less time. Jerry was most likely to be faster than any horse, his legs could reach out 5 feet further than any horse.

Jerry had a couple animal friends at the zoo who had arrived their around the same time Carolyn the fox; Ered fox Daniel the lion with fur 9 inch thick and Harold a hard shell slow turtle that weighed 121 pounds. Jerry was friends with all the animals at the zoo, even the next largest animal at the zoo. The grey tail hippo.

Once in a while Jerry would join Herold for a rinse off in the pool built for large animals. Just for fun they would race across the pool. Although Harold was slow on land he made up for it in the pool. Jerry probably could win every race but since Harold made up for his slowness in the pool. He still was a lot slower than Jerry.

Jerry had other friends but he enjoyed being with Herold. They were best friends.

Auto Pill

AUTO RE-STARTED HIS JOURNEY UP the mountain. 250 more feet he climbed. After 3 hours of continuous climbing Auto reached the flat tops of the mountain. At first there were no trees just grass that was bleached out by the sun.

Auto once again made camp.

This time no fire the sun was hot enough to make same green tea from tea leaves Auto had brought with him.

For food he had packed at the beginning of his journey, crackers; recipe cups, he had put them in the ice. Small jar peanut butter to go with crackers and couple bags of cashews and small bags of chips.

Auto spread the peanut butter of some crackers, dipping the plastic battle in a nearby stream he re-filled it. He drank some with the peanut butter and crackers. Auto tore open a bag of onion flavored chips and munched on them while he decided what direction he would travel. It was a hard decision to make.

After eating half bag of chips Auto decided to travel straight ahead towards the sun east.

Auto left the west side behind him. In a small distance Auto could see the top of trees.

If he could see trees best bet there was a river or stream close by the trees. Auto cut out a walking cane from a spruce tree before his climb.

Auto and back pack and bedroll reached the outer part of a 45 mile wide and 60 mile long forest. A good place for his third camp. The sun was still hanging around shinning threw the forest trees. The trees made good shade from the suns hot rays. Plus Auto had packed a pup tent (small tent). He staked out place to tie down the pup tent. Unfolding it he extended it into a 2 man tent, giving him room for his bed roll & back pack.

Auto bedded down for his second night. Climbing into the tent he closed the tents flap behind him.

A small lantern provided him right to read a map of the top of the mountain and the forest he was in.

Auto had also brought a bow and arrows with him he had herd the forest was full of deer and other eatable animals like rabbits and squirrel. Those were in his food source.

There were others, elk, bear, for large prey, medium tigers and mountain lions small prey squirrel, rabbit and in the streams fish.

It had a pair of microscopic glasses bifocals. He thought he might shoot with his bow and arrow 6 rabbit or squirrel.

Nothing showed up not even a bug. Auto waited until the sun went down; before he quit hunting. Once it was down he unpacked his sleeping gear.

Once settled Auto got out his bow and arrow. He grabbed couple bags of chips and with bow on hand and a bag of arrows on his shoulder Auto went out into the woods hunting deer.

Auto hid behind a rock and waited patiently for a deer to wonder away from the rest of the pack. Non showed. So Auto began looking for rabbits one showed up but before Auto towards the squirrel, the squirrel looked up in the direction of the arrow. He saw it coming his way and quickly jumped off the tree limb, with an acorn in its mouth.

Auto gave up and went back to his campsite where his camping gear, tent, bed roll and backpack were.

Auto climbed into his sleeping bag roll and fell asleep.

Auto was running low on food. Since he did not get anything hunting. He had herd of lumberyard was that cut down trees. They supplied the saw and a blade sharpener.

Auto had used a power saw before. He applied to work for a couple days cutting down trees. The boss man handed him a saw & blade sharpener and said go to it.

Auto cut trees for 3 hours. The boss paid him $4000, Auto thanked him then headed to the west side of the forest where there was a market that bought hunters catch skin them then delayed the animal for meat. He also made dried meat sticks.

Auto bought some deer meat and a couple dried meat sticks; one deer & one squirrel.

Auto liked the deer and ate both the deer and both meat sticks.

The sun reclined behind the trees while the moon raised above the trees.

Auto unrolled his bed roll then climbed in. Hunting waiting for an animal to show was tiresome. Aut laid his head down on a pillow. It was seconds when Auto feel into a deep sleep.

Aut woke at first sun rise. He removed himself from the bed roll. Made a fire out of twigs and leaf, he filled the tin cup full of water and made some coffee. Too early for tea he thought. He put the tin plate on the fire he cooked the remainder of the deer meat for his breakfast.

Auto liked it upon the mountain. He cleared out a space about 3 acres. Then he went to the loggers and cut wood for 5 hours. He was paid $60.00 for his work.

Auto bought 35 logs for 20.00 he paid 5.00 for one of the loggers to take the logs to the 3 acres he had cleared. After 1 month Auto had enough logs to build a log cabin. With mud and rain water Auto stacked the logs atop each other until there were four sides.

Auto had made a knife from stone; he cut out 7 windows. 2 in the front 2 in the back one each side. He also cut out shutters to block out bad weather,

Auto mad two rooms a working room and a sleeping room. He also made a bed from wood and straw. All Auto building took 2 months.

Once the cabin had been built Auto planted a veggie garden. He planted cabbage, lettuce, peas, okra, brussle sprouts, corn, water melon, and muskmelon.

Winter was just around the corner. Auto knew how to can he had done it when he was a boy with his mom.

He made about 50 cans of canned veggies. He still had his bow and arrow and he had shot some deer & rabbit. The veggies and deer & rabbit meat lasted the month. The following month, Auto bought a Remmington long barrel hunting riffle.

He was further away and he did not scare his prey away.

Auto had earned the rights to the 3 acres by squatters, claim if no one claimed it by the end of the year. It was his and the county gave him a deed to the land.

Could get his arrow onto the bowstring the rabbit hopped out of sight.

Auto was discussed; but he thought of giving it one more chance. He looked up into the tree for a squirrel. One was out on a limb collecting acorns. Slowly Auto pulled back the string on the bow; then quickly let it go.

The arrow followed a path Auto went down to mountain to the market. He bought supplies for the winter. The market delivered his supplies the next day.

Auto had some patching up to do some of the logs were water soaked and water beetles were eating the water soaked logs.

Auto had heard about plaster that would hold the logs together.

Auto replaced the logs and applied the plaster over the mud in-between the logs. To Auto's surprise the plaster made the cabin warmer during the winter and cooler during summer.

Auto meets Molley the Mountain Lady. Molley is the first of 20 to follow to climb the mountain.

Auto was at the market when Molley came in for supplies for her cabin she had built by paying workers 25.00 a wk. They took 3 months to build her cabin. They had made her cabin double logs back to back with sheets of wood between 16 logs. Not only was her cabin more sturdy but more weather proofed. The inside was smaller but her cabin was warmly, Molly also had her own mule drawn wagon that pulled her supply's home.

"Mr. Pill would you like for me to take you supply's home?" "That won't be necessary." Auto replied "No trouble. Besides it will be quicker if I did."

Auto thought and finally agreed. He stacked his supplies on her flatbed. It was at his place in no time. Auto offered Molly $10.00 she said she did not need it.

Once a month Molley took Auto's supplies home for him.

Auto and Molly became friends twice a month Auto picked Molleys and planted garden in return for her hauling his supplies to his home.

After one year Molley and Auto decided to change supplies. He had supplies she needed and she had some he needed a couple years passed Molly and Auto became lovers and after 4 years of knowing one another they married. The combined their cabins when it was cold. This place he stayed at Molly's when cold at Molly's they stayed at Auto's place. After 1½ years they had a baby boy. They named Parker.

The boy could not be shifted from one log cabin to the other they decided to build a third cabin in the middle of their lands. It would be the main house. All three lived in it. The other two houses were used as storage and work houses.

This worked out fine since they both loved living on the mountain. Parker became known as the mountain child.

The Middle of the Road

DONALD WAS A MIDDLE OF the road kind of guy. He was not slack in his work but did not have a 100% work ethic.

Donald had plenty of room to expand because of his middle of the road efforts.

Donald was not the only one who was considered a middle of the road guy. Donald's friend were also considered the middle of the road people.

In the world there are all sorts of classes of people. There are in the world 4 different classes the sower to his fellow man that gave him the strength to a long and noteworthy life. Also his love of family gave him strength.

Donald supported his family in everything. He had his older brother Kieth to thank for his support of others in the family.

Donald had come into some cash. An inheritance from Donald's sister that kept his hopes up was named Kathy spelled it with a K instead of a C. Kath had lived in the state of Omaha since she was born never leaving keeping the family heritage alive and well in their home state.

Donald and Kathy is what kept the family in touch with one another they both had a close relationship and when Abbe gave the family their support. It was through them that the family came together.

Robert Alter

ROBERT NEW WHAT HE WANTED to be when he became a working man. Ever since age 7 when he got an erector set for his 6ᵗʰ birthday.

Robert emptied a long rectangular box of crome plated building pieces on to the living room floor piece from ½ to 12 inches in length and ¼ inch wide came tumbling out of the erector set cardboard box along with screws and nuts; that held the metal pieces together.

Robert looked at the instructions and illustration that came with the pieces inside the cardboard box. After a brief study Robert began assembling his first projects with his erector set. It was a 36 inch long by 12 inch wide bridge. Robert was proud of his bridge. His next assembly was a house complete with windows & doors; it even had closet space.

At the end of the year Robert took inventory of the things he had assembled with his erector set. It was not just buildings & bridges, it was also cars and robots and a crane.

There was nothing Robert could not make out of erector set pieces.

Robert had herd of the tinker toys you could do same thing as you could do with erector set pieces; and more.

Robert was going past the toy store when he saw a wind mill made from the tinker toys. A price tag set next to it. It read tinker toy set of 24 for $7.99 Robert reached into his pocket and pulled out 78 cents; not even enough for large candy bar that cost 89 cents. He needed $6.20 more. Robert ran back home. He emptied out his cubby piggy bank $4.17 was all there was, with the 78 cents $4.95. 5 cents short of $5.00. He still needed $3.04. He ask his brother Eddie for the $3.04 "I only have a buck 5 cents." He still was short $1.95 he asked his father, "Okay empty the trash and vacuum the living room rug." "I'll give you $3.00." Probably taxes to be paid Robert vacuumed the floor first then the trash emptied just before night.

Robert ran up the street to the toy store. The owner had closed one minute before Robert arrived "Oh well I will come back tomorrow morning it would be Saturday." Just as Robert turned to go home Mr. Morr saw Robert he knew Robert was there to buy the tinker toys. He opened the door. "Robert, if you have the correct change for the tinker toys I will sell it to you." "I do," said Robert, quickly as he could Robert reached into his pocket and pulled out all the money he had. "The correct change!" Robert thanked Mr. Morr then ran home. He could not wait until he got to his room he emptied all 24 pieces out on the living room rug. They tumbled out like the pieces in the erector set did, there were round thick pieces with holes; long 6 inch pole like pieces and short, the had slots in the end for triangle shaped pieces. He used them as flags there was also long, short, and square pieces that bent. Robert looked at an instruction booklet. It illustrated some things he could make with the tinker toys. Robert made a couple before going to bed.

Tomorrow was Sunday, after church he could work with the tinker toys and see what he could make.

Robert ran home as soon as church was over. While he opened the box of tinker toys Robert he realized that he could mix the tinker toys and the erector set pieces. Something tinker toy maker did not realize.

When they heard about Robert mixing the two, (tinker toys and erector set). They offered him money to show them some of the things he had made with the two. It was $500.00 a lot of money. Robert agreed to show them a few things for $500.00.

Once the tinker toy company learned some things that could be made mixing the two the erector set component & the tinker toy company made an agreement to combine the two and sell them in a 50 piece set. They would name Erector & Tinker Toy box. The split the profits. The also gave Robert 5% of all sells.

Robert said no to the offer. And made an offer of his own. Supply me with one set a month 12 a year and 5% of sells made from other things made them buy both erector set & tinker toys. They agreed to Robert's offer. They knew there would be advancement coming out of the erector set and tinker toy boxes.

Breakfast at My Apartment

BREAKFAST AT MY APARTMENT IS not always at the same time; but always before noon.

Breakfast at my apartment is not always the same either. Take today for example; a good meal to start off the day. First before or during breakfast a hot cup of coffee; or Java in to the South.

Once I've had a coffee and sometimes glass of water, I begin cooking. Today a thick center cut pork chop breaded, two eggs over easy sometimes hard. If potatoes & candice up into a skillet and make either, home fries, fried potatoes; or mash them, put egg & flower & milk in a bowl mix, then smash potato into bowl of flower egg & milk.

Potato patties, whip up some brown or mushroom gravy pour into gravy bowl with spout. Fry potato cake in skillet for about 2 minutes or until golden brown, add powder sugar, not much. Crack two or three eggs. Cook as desired fried easy; hard; light scrambled or hard scrambled. If desired bowl of brown cream of wheat or just plain; or oats; plain or sugar.

Instead of the center cut pork chop; crispy strips of bacon around 3 or 4. With eggs if a light breakfast or breakfast on the run brown toast toasted light or dark. With butter natural or saturated, sometimes a squint of sugar honey or honey straight from the sap of a tree, or beehive.

Most always a healthy meal if not in mood for breakfast a couple slices of toast with coffee regular grind.

Breakfast at my apartment when company arrives (hardly ever) I might add a powder sugar cone or hot apple or cherry pie, or cinnamon role with bear honey comb straight from a bees home.

Most of the time breakfast is before 9:00 AM or 900 hour military time government.

Today I has set out a center cut 1 inch thick, fried to a golden brown served with baby potato sliced and fried. Bowl of corn pops or cornflakes. Sweet 2 go milk in cup, not glass one light fried egg (starting diet to lose weight or lower cholesterol.

When I have fruits like mush melon, strawberry's, grapes or fried apple pie on cherry, tie will have them with glass of juice, lemon, grape fruit; grape juice or coconut juice.

When no one around but myself couple cups of coffee or chocolate milk; maybe if I have gone to store late in the month when money scarce and have no means to get any a search of the items; breakfast. I might or might not come up with a meal. So coffee & toast it is. Maybe a fruit like peach, strawberry, apple or whatever is in the fridge.

Today I have several breakfast meals I can make. I choose the breaded pork chop.

Well medication alarm going off time to take my meds and shut off that annoying alarm on my phone with only 7 minutes change of my choice of breakfast to help my diet plans. Coffee, bowl peaches and my visit from nurse @ 10:00 AM. Or 10 hundred hours, gov. time

The Eagle That Ruled The Forrest

SEPARATED FROM HIS FAMILY WHILE in flight Stivers a brown dark orange Eagle; got tired from flying around searching for his family saw an empty space to land on the Ohio River in northern Pittsburgh Pennsylvania. Stivers went on a downward flight where he landed in the empty space. On one side was the Ohio River; when he turned to his back side a forest.

Not a good swimmer Stivers chose the forest he began walking, he still did not feel like flying.

Passing a line of birch trees Stivers walked deeper into the forest. Past walnut trees; birch then oak. By the time he passed the oak he decided to walk towards the elm trees tomorrow.

Stivers looked around for a pile of leaves;

Stivers eyeballed a pile of cedar leaves. They had turned brown and yellow a stage where they were soft. Stivers pilled the cedar leaves in a pile as long as his body. He then mashed them around until they were soft, he then bent over to them until they they he had completely laid down. Comfortable Stivers closed his eyes. It was only 1 minute until was sleeping.

Stivers wake when the first sunrise appeared threw the trees in the forest.

Stivers flapped his wings vigorously as he threw out his chest. Looking left then right Stivers then stepped out from the pile of leaves he slept on. After flapping a few more times Stivers took flight into the air just 2 feet above the forest trees it was the line of oak he was about to overcome. That blew him down. The winds they caused was to strong Stivers landed under a small oak that he later climbed out on a limb and took flight from. He did not fly high but it was high enough.

Stivers strong wings is why he was able to withstand the forest winds.

It was his extra strong eye sight that got Stivers into places no other eagle so go. It was his ability to tilt his wings and fly threw a narrow passage.

These things was special traits that no other eagle possessed.

Stivers could spot the smallest thing from his high places and was able to pick up all sizes of creatures and foods from a high place that he was able to gain a high speed and and latch onto a object and fly off to his nest with it.

Stivers has been flying the once two forest; but now one since he was a young eagle. Eagle had been around the forest for a while he could go where no other eagle could. He was still one of the quickest; one of the most knowledgeable of all the buds or creatures that made the forest their home.

Only one other could feel Stivers traits that was of another eagle that was 2 years. That eagle was his older brother Steave. It was only because Steave was the elder and had learned the forest a little more Steave and Stivers were the two eagles that kept the forest up by making sweeps through the forest. But Steave speed was a little slower but his knowledge about the forest was advance.

The Match

J ENNEY WAS A YOUNG LADY of 17 years of age, most of her friends were married, Jenny thought she had better get busy finding a man to marry. It took her ½ years to mail her a man. She wanted her wedding on the 1st January, that way she would remember her anniversary when she celebrated the New Year.

So next year around December 10 she would plan her marriage for Jan 1. That would be perfect, start off the year getting married, then every January 1; not only would she be celebrating New Years she would be having celebration of her anniversary.

Jenny got a hold of eligible men, prospects for dating. It was about 40 men in the area that were her age or younger, she had no quarrel about male being younger than herself. Jenny glanced up & down the list she got to prospect number 7, 2 inches taller than her; she stood 5 ft ½ inch "maybe"? she thought, she scrolled on down the list of eligible men No. 14 kind of got her attention. He was a mixed color of hair blond and red, his hair was fully grown out. Seemed like he was going to be a red head. Time would tell. Maybe? It would turn blonde because of the sun would bleach out the red hair.

Jenny was single; she is 21. She thought it was about time she found herself a man that she could date for about a year. That would gave her enough time to assess him for marriage later on. About a year and a half down the road. It is June now half way through Jenney looked further down the list; until she reached Number 31 another prospect. He was broad shouldered, like a football player might be? Large biceps; also like a football player, and had her color of eyes; hazel with a hint of green. She thought that was cute.

She had only got to 34 when she saw another guy she might go for 1 only 6 men left; they were all men past age 21, she choose two out of the 6th one tall and slim large hands; the other short and pudgy.

Jenny had chosen 7 men from the list of 40, she wrote down all on a paper then tore the paper until there were 7 pieces.

She mixed them in a tin box; mixing them and shaking the box 7 times one for each man. She picked out three pieces of paper with a name on each. The first was James the blond red head; the second was the slim tall guy, Andy the third was the guy with broad shoulder and large biceps guy.

Jenney put the three pieces of paper with James one with Andy's name and the last with guy's name she mixed them like she did with the 7 names. She reached in and picked one name. She unfolded the paper. She had picked Andy that would be her man.

She had 11 months to get ready for her marriage. Jenny first had to persuade Andy to accept her as his bride to be. Andy was going to be at the Indy 500 in three days she bought a ticket; to the race it was a long shot she would find Andy; lucky her she had bought a ticket in the same section and even the same raw. She glanced at the picture she had of Andy.

Andy was three seats down from her. He was going to the concession stands. She followed and when he had bought his food and drinks she jumped out and nudged him. Oh! "Excuse me." "I'm sorry; she said, "Can I help you carry you food back to your seat? looks like you have a hand full.

They went back to their seats. And was surprised when Jenney went to her seat only three seats down from his.

Andy traded seats with the lady next to Jenney. Now; are you satisfied? "This is no accident we were setting so close" Okay what's your reason to get use together?" "I have plans for use. She answered. "Yea!" "What?" he said.

Marriage in 6 month. "What," he said; in a loud voice. "I am going to persuade you to marry me in 6 months; "Oh no." I'm not." We will see Jenny said. They watched the rest of the race. It was a in the 7th lap 40 altogether. It turned out they were both rooting for the same race car driver.

That was odd. Jenny had took a bus to the race track. Andy offered her a ride home. The beginning of their relationship that would lead to Jenny's plan to be married on January 1st, and it did happen. They both live in a ranch home 2 miles from the Ind 500. Every year they go to the place they first met, and on the 1st January 1st they celebrate the New Year and their honeymoon.

Colby and Darlean

C OLBY MEET DARLEAN AT NEVADA Valley missile base Fort Harrison. They both were training to be scientist on the Starlite space ship, it was headed to Mars a satellite that was launched on a path that was kept secret by the N.A.S.A. teams.

While on the space ship Colby took samples of debris floating space. Colby to get it a name. He could remember. After tagging some of the debris, he stuffed it in lead coated canteens 6 foot high 3 foot wide. The debris tagged sometimes was equal in items collected. Items that more like in natural state.

There was debris that was broken up and when broken were different, that was not all but most of Colby's job duties.

Darlean had other duties, duties of security, setting up alarms making passwords for certain areas on ship. Most of Darlean's job was done in a security area. She worked from her own space; sending out vibrations to other parts of the ship. Places she has never been nor ever will be. Darlean was one of the top computer experts in the world. She knew how to get from one computer to another by short wave radio; by Amazon to blink to attack. To google to the old type where you hol to use a program call cobbe; cobbe was a system of different size mark lengthwise but width nets the same. It was a system of symbols and letters and numbers. That when arranged in a specific order would convert into a message from the other person to present people.

Cobbe has not been used for a couple centuries. 20 or 40 years, back in early 20's.

Colby checked out and went home. Darlean stayed on site a little longer she needed to make sure her job areas were safe and locked down before she headed home. Everything she had checked was locked down.

Darlean pulled into her home at 7.09 pm she clicked the garage door opener it opened driving into the garage she checked the garage door lock. Darlean was tired she had a long day. She made a salami or rye with dill pickle, poured a glass of her favorite soda, squirt. Setting down on the sofa with her legs tacked under her on the cushion. Darlean picked up the remote control. Hit channel select 12 the evening news was on a car on Ventura Boulevard had crashed into a city bus.

Darlean fell asleep while the weather was on; during commercial she closed her eyes on in secounds was sleeping like a lamb.

Colby had been asleep for hours, he would be waking up soon. When he does Darlean will be & he will be having breakfast together.

Darlean is a pretty good cook when it comes down to making a tasty a breakfast meal. Her favorite meal to make is cornbread and scrambled light eggs with bacon bits spread over French toast with maple syrup. A cup of hot coffee to top of the breakfast plate.

Once breakfast done, a trip to the forest where a water stream flows down into maple trees that lay on the ground.

Darlean searches in the back pack for a colorful brown and green bananas for a light snack.

After digging around for 5 minutes, she finds the banana, but it has been squashed. She scrapes off the banana from the peeling and eats it. She is still hungry but that will do until Colby returns with better food.

Colby has brought back 5 bags of groceries it is enough for at least 5 day for 3 people. Since there is only Darlean Colby 5 will due.

Darlean looks in the full bags to see what Colby has brought back. A couple meat beefsteak, small honey ham and bacon. Also macaroni red potatoes and green beans. Two loafs of wheat bread, a box of Colby cheese, enough for macaroni and noodle dinners.

The month about over soon Colby & Darlean will get their government checks they will be able to stock the refrigerator for at least 3 weeks of food.

Soon Colby and Darlean will be going an adventure together a place in the jungle (forest like any other place but a find is soon to be discovered by Colby and Dean a place in the forest no one has ever been. Perhaps now finds will be found.

The Girl at the Race Track

OCCASIONALLY, MY FAMILY AND I go to the car racing. Once in a while, we might go to a horse race at rived Downs in Kentucky and I reside in Bloomington Indiana. Almost a straight line through Kentucky to Cincinnati Ohio, on 75.

On the way to Bloomington we stop and enjoy a couple horse races one in Lexington and one in Covington Kentucky.

Before getting to either race track we stop at a dinner on our way to the tracks.

Both dinners change menus daily. So we never know what we will be eating when we stop in.

So we do not set our appetite on anything special. Like a roast pot or a lamb and potato pot roast. We do not even plan on a simple baloney or ham sandwich.

Sometimes a frank and fry meal just fine works sometime we might have a big appetite. This year we thought we might go farther south we had heard about Datona Saw Beachours and liked what we saw. After saving about 2,000.00 we first bought a used van. Some backpacks gashed up the van, locked down the house and put security lock around it then headed south. We were already in the south we just went deeper.

Breaking camp every 100 '25 miles, sometimes every 45 miles.

Both me and Miss like dancing and just for the fun.

Pulling out of a camping with in southern Kentucky we wave good bye to KY for a planned vacation of 2 month. That was about how much longer the racing circuit had left; not just car also our favorite horse races. Crossing into Tennessee from KY around Nashville. We stop for a quick soda and chips heading in an eastern to southern route we drive on to Chattanooga. A long trip we slay at the Red Roof Inns for 2 nights to freshen up.

The Inn has summer clothing in the lobby. The weather has gotten warmer the family buys shorts, short sleeve shirts.

After we arrange back packs suit cases and bedding camping style, we manage to stuff in cooking gear to cook in while on the road, plus a few groceries.

We decide to slick on to the Alabama-Georgia borders all the way to & all a hose.

With most of the trip south behind us a needed rest stop to freshen up. This time stop in 5 hours not 3. With only Florida left in our southern journey we have 2 more stops to make maybe only one. Jamestown and Gainesville before hitting Jacksonville, Daytona close by. After a night in Jamestown, we head in direction of Daytona sliding into St Petersburg Florida our last stop until Daytona.

Before the race begins in two more days, we decide to take in some sun and find a beach somewhere close. We drive down further south to the cope code area take about a 4 hour swim. Check into one more hotel then after a short breakfast drive on to Daytona.

Pulling into a parking lot near the race track we park in lot 3 space 20.

We enter race track at gate 19. Ginifer, my wife, forgot to mention her name, get a room. We get another. The race is getting ready to begin. The girls went to concession and brought loaf hotdogs meats and sodas with a mix of chips, Doritos to snack or during a grew some 300 miles of racing approximately.

We each pick a horse and stick with it making our own bets.

A fun trip it was win with the long traveling which would be longer on our way home.

We all were excited about going to Daytona.

The race is going to start, everyone has placed their bets, Ted Williams first out of starting gate the first mile he clock a 9:33, 21. He holds his lead for 8 laps; then Winston Reed pulls ahead by 1.3 seconds then 10 seconds on top 7 Reed hold his lead to lap 17; back and forth Reed Williams; Reed; Williams both loose their lead in 15 21st lap.

The race ends 25th lap with neither Reed nor Williams in top 10. The winner Miss Debra Heinze the daughter of Mr. Hienze Soup.

All around the country both in horse racing and car racing the women are dominating the tracks.

Breaking All Boundaries

EBBIE IS AN OWNER OF a lot of land of 155 acres. The land is not equal in bottom soil. None has the same quality as any of the others. The properties are adjacent to one another, stocked 14x8. Debbie wants to plant vegetables randomly but none of the 14x8 acres match. There are too many variables that creates barriers. Lot one, she wants to plant sweat corn, & white corn. When she plants the white corn next to the dark yellow sweat corn; the white corn takes on some of the yellow's color. Not only does the white corn turn yellowish the yellow corn becomes lighter.

In the next lot beside the white corn is a green vegetable, dark in color some of this color transferred to the white corn.

Some is also transferred to the lot 4 where the tip is touching lot 5 it transfers the color of baby red tomatoes to the next field. Through the process of color shifts. Creating a yellow cauliflower instead of the intended white cauliflower.

This crossing of colors transfer a dark color to light in color red a dark color. The crossing of color properties is not creating a developing vegetables not healthy. The only thing it does disrupt is color barriers. (Boundaries)

Besides breaking color barriers the mixing of vines weaving in and out of one another and tree trunks disrupts the natural flow of one plants properties to another of the same. Taking the natural healthy qualities out of its original state.

Boundaries are looked over when a scientist searches for new healing properties.

Boundy crossing is nothing new especially in the medical searches for new healing medicines.

Some barriers boundaries have blockages to prevent one from crossing over a barrier or boundary.

Some are boundaries made for protection from harm. Climbing or crawling or breaking through boundaries with protection from all health, a boundary with no protection from harm can destroy one self. The crossing can cause a weakness letting in bacteria that destroys instead of creating a stronger person of objects.

Farmer Debbie determined to be a modern day farmer. The crossing of boundaries in her case has proved to be beneficial. Instead of creating a crossing over of destruction her crossing have helped the healthy properties. Making her vegetables healthier. Once she researched remained bad properties; the vegetables are growing taller under the color barriers crossing had no effect. The changing was that of mixing badly into the good.

If you are satisfied with vegetable growth the way it was tended to be then I would suggest removing some of the lands natural giving properties before disrupting a plants natural order.

Debbie's research has helped her and the vegetables are of best quality. Debbie has hired help. One person per section. She fills that one person will know their planter best. They are the ones who will grow and nurture their personal plants.

Breaking all boundaries can lessen the healthy factor in plants, removing a property might make a person sick or the property removed might be just what you needed to improve quality of vegetable.

Probably better if you do not cross or remove anything but perhaps creating a boundary between or a safety space between one vegetable to another the way no natural particles or part of all Debbie's vegetables has grown to their fullest. It is first picking. Each planter picks vegetable from the ground in large baskets.

Debbie is now faced with marketing her vegetable from her gardens. She was crews who pick in each growth section. She hopes to have a more profitable good and also a healthy pick.

Debie has taken record of all vegetables planted and she has recorded sales of each production after taking an inventory, Debby finds a profit that makes the whole deal.

The Woman from Down the Road

WINTER HAS ARRIVED; THE FIRST snow fall of the season is just a little snow flurries not even enough to make a difference. They quite as fast as they began. Debbie life every other morning went to the curb to get the morning paper. A shadow fell at Debbie's feet.

Debbie's eyes looked outwards and down the road. They followed the shadow until it stopped at the foot of an elderly lady. She was reaching out her hand to Debbie.

Hesitantly, Debbie reached her hand out.

Both hands stretched out, Debbie leaned in a little closer. The elderly lady withdrew slightly.

Debbie wondered why? Why did she reach her hand out only to withdraw it.

Okay Debbie thought "I will bite." Debbie reached out a little closer. The elderly lady again slightly withdrew her hand again. Debbie was getting a little angry. "This time." "I will sludge into her hand. I bet we will connect then?" Debbie began a count, 1, 2, 3, when she reached 4 Debbie gave over hand another big plunge towards the woman's hand.

Finally the both hands come together. Debbie felt a big jerk. The elderly lady pulled Debbie her way. Debbie felt something it was like a flash of lightning had flashed across a tile floor room; or a glass floor room.

Debbie's body shook from fear. It was though she had gone through a field of lightning rays.

Debbie's eyes had closed just as the flash occurred. She re-opened them not long after the flash. It was as though she hand entered another world.

Building off in the near distance appeared. Debbie did not remember them being there, on the opposite side, a bar; a jail house; and a grocery store. It was weird. Debbie thought neither were they there another weird thing was 3 children waving at her; it was as though they were not there reaching out a Debbie. Only they were, and Debbie was at them. They turned away from her and kept waiving their hand like they were saying come on, the children were about ½ block away from Debbie. Like with the old lady they were saying come here.

Debbie ran toward the three child she clutched onto their hands, they lead her down the road not half block; not a block no did they lead her one mile. They lead her to the old ladies home down the road, Debbie had seen the house before. She could not think of where it might be?

Debbie perhaps it was a home she saw while walking to the store? Debbie had no time to worry about it know she was busy at home adding a room and putting in a tool shed for the tools she uses for her lawn care.

She thought since she had seen it before she will probably see it another time?

The night was passing soon the sun would be rising. Debbie could not wait because she liked working on the garden (flower) she had planted some Silcocks and some Zailia's. Those were her favorite flowers.

Some times when Debbie was working in her flower garden or other gardens. The lady down the street would appear, Debbie has gotten to the point to ignore the woman down the street. But still she wonders why she keep on appearing.

Debbie has hired someone to see who it is, why the woman appears around her all the time?

They find out the lady down the street is related to she is her great aunt who has a gift for her and it is from other in the family's trusts. Debbie is relieved and makes the detective she had hired to tell the lady down the street she would like to meet with her and talk about their family's ties.

Maybe they can do a family search? And Debbie asked her what her name was, and is she on mom's side or dad's side. She agrees and Debbie goes down on the street to meet her. Her name is? It is Aunt Milly from your mom side of the family.

Debbie & Milly meet and become friends. They have been missing a lot of good things and are going to make them up.

The Little Sailor

KEVIN MILLER SINCE HIS FIRST time on the water in a river boat has had a deep love for the water, he would rather be on a boat in a river lake ocean or sea, than to be on land; living in a cold damp empty house.

Kevin learned his first not as a boy just like all boys. The loop twist around pull not. I'm speaking of the not learned to tie your shoe. Commonly known as a bowtie.

Not was Kevin's first that led to a variety of nots Kevin had learned during his life time most he learned on sailing adventures around the world. Kevin had made a life as a sailor and during that time sailed every large body of water from lake to a river to an ocean to the sea.

When sailing Kevin had learned just about every sailing job there was. From being a swaby mopping deck; to a dishwasher to a cook to a flag raiser.

There was no job Kevin could not do on any kind of sailing vessel from a dingy to a 7 story crew slinnor. That included pouring Champaign for the officers in the mess hall, when on a body of water Kevin did not hurt for any work he would earn his way doing one of the many chores on a sailing vessel. That even included repairing the ship when damaged.

The little sailor got his nick name The Little Sailor from his small physical body. Not a tall man, nor a heavy man was Kevin. Thin as bamboo stick small; not like a midget but only 4'8" 132 pounds and no muscular part on his body Kevin earned his name as the little sailor who did a sailors job.

Because Kevin liked being on the water he made a career of being a sailor. Even after military duties on a Pt boat when other sailors talked of the little sailor everyone knew it was Kevin Miller. He was the only one in the fleet that was called the little sailor. When he began sailing on his own he kept the nick name The Little Sailor. By keeping it he was able to make friendships all around the world. Kevin had made an impression among all sailor's private military, and even the most valued of all professions. The fisherman with his little dingy. Kevin could even work a house boat not only downstream but with a large pole push it up stream if the boat came undone or damage Kevin new how to restore it back to tiptop shape or at least to floating on water safely.

All these strength Kevin used when he began a career as a ship builder.

Kevin started with 10 fishing boats. Then added speed boats then Cabin Cruisers then Ocean Liners.

Kevin's ship building business grew and he expanded to 10 ship building companies. The largest in the world.

When someone wanted a ship boat or even a small dingy they knew Kevin was the best ship builder ever except for NetW9.

When needed Kevin will help others build ships.

When on vacation he will sail on the finest of ships. His fare paid because when he was aboard everyone knew they were on a well-built ship. Kevin not even using his name Kevin but going by The Little Sailor name everyone knew they were in good company. They also when on vacation looked for the insignia that was called The Little Sailor. It was a round desk with a sailor carved on it in a blue coat and setting in the front of a sail boat directing the boat in the direction he wanted to go.

The sailor also had on a white cop in the shape of a cooks cop but brown instead of white. The sailor on the insignia also wore knee high black boots. There was no mistaken the insignia was that of a sailor steering or giving direction to. That insignia became the symbol of Kevin Miller's ship building company.

Vinnie

A stone mason in Warez New Mexico hounds on hot steamy metal into the shape of a horse's foot. He is putting the finishing touches on the right hind foot the last of silvers, a silver colored horse foot. He is about to finish he pounds softly so not to harm the foot of silver. Silver is happy he is finishing the last shoe.

Vinnie finishes Silver, he leads her back to the barn with the other horses. 3 others are already fitted. 4 to go. Vinnie shoes one horse every 2 days. 6 more days of shoeing horses. Vinnie charges $10.00 a foot plus 5.00 each whole piece of metal used on one shoe. A full shoeing can be $45.00 to $60.00 Vinnie pays $3.00 for a slab of metal. 2 foot by 1 foot, plenty to make a horse shoe.

Vinnie closes shop at 6:00 pm all metal boxed up in a storage bend. Vinnie walks over to another bend he removes the buckets of metal; a blow torch; a heavy metal hammer.

Walking over to a horses stall he removes 2 horses. He measures both horses feet front to back side to side. He records the measurements. He goes to a oven he made of metal puts in a scoop of coal. The oven gets hot, Vinnie heats up one of the 2 inch pieces of metal. He starts pounding it with the metal hammer.

Slowly the metal flattens to 1 inch. He puts it in a vat of water cooling it off he re-heats it then pounds on it more until ½ inch thick. Cools it a second time then hammers on it again. Finally it flattens to the desired thickness, about ⅛th inch. With a steel spike and another heating he pounds the holes for the spikes to go into 4 holes each side of the shoe. It is time for the shoeing at the horse he set the shoes at. Vinnie goes to the stable gets the horse he fitted first strike in the back. Four or five more than a spike to the right or left whichever he chooses. Then the opposite side moving on up to the toes where the last two spikes are hammered into.

The owner leaves $60.00 on the cashier's box. Then leads the horse to his home slowly by riding it home.

Vinnie takes a second horse from the stables. Puts it in a separate stall.

Repeating the heating of the metal, measuring the horse's feet heating and cooling of the metal into shape. Pounding it down to a desired thickness, shaping it into the shape of the horse's feet.

Twice a day Vinnie makes horse shoes. $120.00 a day or times 6 days or $7.20 a week. Or $2,880.00 a month. $34,560 a year.

Hard labor work but worth it by the end of the year.

Vinnie's stalls can support only 10 horses at a time. He has to go to the field lasso a horse and restall the stall the previous horse was in. 6 days work done on a Sunday after church. A catch of 20 to 30 horses depending on how many are in the area. Each horse must be adult a standard set by ranchers in town.

Vinnie has grown and needs to hire some help another shoe-er and another to round up horses, but most of all Vinnie needs to find buyers for the horses he has showed.

Benny has rented a sign post in the center of town thus he list kinds of horses showed cost of metal price of horse & price for showing.

Sometimes a company will buy 20 or 30 horses showed then sometimes only two or three only. Vinnie has also hired an accountant book keeper to keep track of sales made, materials bought hours worked money in account and debits occurred during business. Once the accountant does his job Vinnie can count up his profits, which ends up being used for house hold expenses.

Vinnie might end up with $400.00 of free money. That Vinnie uses most for business expenditures. Leaving only $200.00 or $300.00 for pleasure.

Paula and Chuck the Arangatang

Paula was seven years old entering into the 2nd grade along with the rest of the first graders she had started school with.

The first week was show and tell week. Students could bring an object they had sometime during the summer months. Paula had been to the city zoo the weak before school started. She last visited the arangatangs before going home. Altogether there were 5 arangatangs. Each one had a specific color of collar around its wrist. A name board was at the entrance of the arangatangs exhibit. I'd named each according to the color.

Chuck was Black collar. Paula looked around she first spotted Ruby; she was climbing a birch tree, Paula scanned around for the others. Hanging from a shelf was Ruby sister Debbie. She was hanging by her long bush tail. Paula searched for the other arangatangs.

In the play room climbing on a vine, only two more to find Chip and Chuck.

Paula walked on thru the arangatang exhibit. She passed the monkey bars; then passed by a slide Chip was there sliding down a spiral slide. That left Chuck.

It was not long after she found Chip she had discovered he had already been on the twisting shake. He was going over to the red white and blue ball in the corner.

Paula reached the ball before Chuck. She grabbed it, then bounced it up and down Chuck extended his long red fury arms out; then wiggled his fingers and wrist. It was like he was saying throw me the ball.

Paula bounced the red white and blue ball a couple more times then tossed it across the room to Chuck. Chuck caught it on its 3rd bounce.

Chuck bounced the ball twice then threw it back to Paula.

After playing for a while Paula and Chuck knew they would be friend forever.

Paula approached the arangatang. Arangatang trainer. I would like to take Chuck home as my pet. Terry the trainer filled out the pet adoption papers and Paula with a leather leach led Chuck to her car, once back to Paula's. She led Chuck to his new home.

She had made a play room for him and her to play in. Chuck took to it like he had been living there a long time.

Paula had not had a bite to eat all day. And she bet neither did Chuck. She made them both a bowl of Honey Dats.

Paula was now in the 8th grade her last year in pre school; Chuck was now 4 years old. Counting from the day she brought him home.

Chuck liked Paula very much but he was missing companionship with another like himself.

Paula noticed Chuck was lonely.

Paula took Chuck by the hand and they both went to the Pet Shop. The Pet Shop overseer was not the same as it was when Paula took Chuck home. Chuck checked out the females in the third cage was a female that took a liking to Chuck and he to her.

Together all three walked out of the pet store. I think we will call you Kelly.

Paula was now the owner of two arangatangs Chuck and Kelly.

The Jewels

PAMALA BRUCE KENNETH AND JAMAL were the 4 members of the Jewel family. Pamala called Pam was the mother; Bruce a muscular man of 6 foot 2 was the father; Bruce owner of a logging company with 10 employees; each with a specific assigned job. Mike Shoester was the manager. Joana secretary; Kevin in charge of keeping up saws. Peter truck driver (tools) Jimmy Slade tree lumber separator. Yen Marketing Supper. John, Leroy; Donnie; Dave and Mary Union employees.

Those are the families and employee workers of the Jewels and Co.

A call in the office would get you Joana; she took your order of pieces, type of wood; if weatherized address where to deliver.

Kevin and Jimmy Slade cut lumber even though Kevin sharpened saws he helped the cutting down and cutting to specified length and width. Bruce and Pamala were the social relations reps. They worked with clients and over seed their needs. Making sure their orders were filled like they specified.

John, Leroy, Donnie Dave and Mary union members who worked on special orders. Man by large orders for construction jobs.

Peter and Jimmy-went to a forest preferable one with a variety of trees.

Peter and Jimmy approached an oak tree. They checked their orders. They had 3 orders for lumber of oak. They decided to use the two man saw.

Peter pulled while Jimmy pushed. At first it was slow but the further into the oak the push & pull went faster. Jimmy and Peter got in rhythm the new when it was push and pull time. After pushing and pulling the two man saw for 20 minutes the oak fell to the ground. After a break up 2 minutes Jimmy got out the power saw. He sharpened its teeth (cutting edge.) Jimmy pulled the pull cord and the power saw began humming. The chain of sharpened teeth went through the thick tree limbs at the base of the tree before they cut up the thin branches they went to a second tree and cut it down the third tree was cut down the same manner.

After all three oaks were cut up they took out their rulers and measured the length, to measure the circumference they used a thin rope of turns roped it around the tree then measured the length of the turns. Once they had the oak measured they stacked it in a 36x1" of 24 then they split it in 3 different stacks. Two stacks went to the Bill and Mary's Inns. A second stack went to Bills, he was building a storage bend. The last stack went to the oak lounge. That was a day's work the following day was porch tree day. After a 2 mile trip they came to a forest full of porch. The cut it in 2x4. The Jewels had chosen the days of the week they would cut down a selected type of tree for wood.

The Jewels had been in business for a year when they decided to expand and build a company in the next county.

Pam became the CEO of the second Jewels Lumber Bruce shipped the inventory to Jewel shop no 2, Pam signed for it. Pam had hired 6 people to help do the work at the second Jewels Lumber.

Tom, Danny and Harry 3 brothers Sherry, Dottie and Sue the female employees.

They helped load lumber onto carts while the men loaded them onto delivery truck.

The third year Pam & Bruce's income profits allowed them to open a 3rd Jewels Lumber.

They opened the third shop in Buffalo New York even though their main inventory grew in warm areas.

In Buffalo pine was the wood of choice and there were several pine forest around, perch and walnut grew in Buffalo. With the three stores, the Jewels earned a comparable income.

They hired an accountant to keep book on their expenditures and inventory.

The Jewelry Box

Sharon & Lilly; sisters share a bed room at their home. The top half is Sharon's jewelry the bottom half is Lilly's.

Sharon has 3 broaches one with a cream color of eagle. With its wings spread. One silver with her mother picking silver tulips the third is grey tent with copper flowers slowing on a vine.

Other jewelry Sharon has in her top half is a diamond ring; a nickel ring; a pearl necklace.

Sharon and Lilly are twins and they like to imitate each other. Lilly does have some jewelry Sharon does not have and the same for Sharon.

Sometimes they borrow each other's jewelry (the jewelry the other does not have.

One evening Sharon borrowed Lilly's gold necklace.

She had borrowed it without telling Lilly. The very next day Sharon noticed the bracelet was missing. She inquired about it to Sharon. Sharon replied "I do not know where it is." Lilly thought that someone one came in the house while they were out. She was going to call the police.

Sharon said give it time it will show up. "Okay!" Lilly hold Sharon.

Sharon was relieved when Lilly agreed to wait a couple days. The two days would give Sharon time to search for the bracelet she had misplaced.

It had to be in one of the rooms in the house.

Sharon began a search; Lilly was out for the next 4 hours. Sharon began in the bed room they shared. She pulled the blanket off the bed no bracelet, she pulled the top sheet of still no blanket no bracelet yet. Next she pushed over the bed no bracelet under the bed on the floor. Sharon next search was the dresser; she moved everything around a couple times the bracelet was not on the dresser. Sharon had been in her mother & fathers bed room to change linen. She searched their bed; their dresser; even the trash can. Sharon's home was only one floor. At least she did not have to climb stairs.

Sharon searched every room; the kitchen; the living room the den even the hallway.

She would wait until the next day for a second search. Sharon went to bed early so morning would come fast. It did and Sharon skipped her breakfast so she could search for the bracelet.

Her search began outside at the steps of the front door down the sidewalk that lead to the end of their property.

No bracelet on the sidewalk. Sharon step off the sidewalk, to the left. She kicked the grass around as she made her way to the left property line. Still no bracelet.

Sharon went to the right side kicked around the grass nowhere around was the bracelet.

Once Sharon had searched the front sides a back of the house. It was getting late luck for Sharon Lilly was not thinking about.

The bracelet was nowhere on the property; at least Sharon had not found it.

Sharon had gone to the clock store it was 4 blocks away. She bought an alarm clock. She inquired to the clerk if he had found a silver bracelet? He answered with a soft voice "No."

Sharon knew not where to search; she gave up. She went home.

That evening she was preparing what she was going to where to school? Sharon was all dressed. She had one more thing to do. She had to put on jewelry. She started putting on ear rings she then took out; of her half; the top half a different bracelet. While putting it on her wrist she dropped it, the bracelet landed in the compartment she kept her necklace. She had a compartment full of necklaces. Shuffling them around looking for one to match while shuffling her necklaces around Sharon spotted the bracelet she had misplaced.

She took it from the necklace compartment put in Lilly's bracelet compartment, then closed the lid.

Lilly come in and was looking for another bracelet. It was caught on something. Lilly pulled until it was loose.

It was the bracelet that Sharon had lost.

The Bridge to Nowhere

OUT IN A FIELD A road leads up to a brick tunnel. It stands all alone with snow on the top of 4 proofs two are flat one at a diagonal about 4 foot high another that resembles a roof; but not looks like a piece of wood laying up against the bridge. Off to the right trees in the background; then a white & gray, turning blacker.

Looking directly at the bridge at the top symbol a flat head to a sided hammer and a flat head one side and the other pointed to and of like a pick. They cross each other about midway.

Under the picks is about 4 lines of writing. Cannot make out of line second one a name Christina all in capital letters two more line too small for my eyes to tell what it says. The last line a date 1718-1719; either one I think the later.

Looking into the bridge in darkness. Hard to tell if you can come out on the other side. If so where? A division of country or county a kind of scary another world? My guess county? Or city or to nowhere?

My guess also by those who can read the writting kows what is it the other end, if there is an end at all?

A little to the left you can see more snow; also higher left a tree branch. Maybe an elm or maple? Green leaves in winter. Snow clings to the leaves. One can only imagine if there is a wind. If so not much; no leaves are falling from the trees. Or snow, nor are the branches swaying, it is like all is frozen in time. No activity of anything. No bird flying around and not even a bug crawling in the ground or up a tree. Approaching the bridge might be hesitant to travel into or through the bridge. Or even around.

It would be my inclination to pass on by. Not so give it a second thought never even come anywhere near the bridge ever again.

But then curiosity might lure you to enter in check it out. Or at least read the description and get knowledge why it was built. No river does it go over. No drop of land does it go over. Why it was even built. Another question to the bridges existence of the bridge that stands alone is who built it. What was their reason for building it? No river no droppage no average of anything except the road that travels into it. Perhaps it was built to honor someone. Judging by the name on it CHRISTINA and the year 1718 or 19. It was built to HONNOR CHRISTINA in that year. Then maybe not honoring CHRISTINA at all. Maybe someone choose that specific name in the bridge? One thing for sure it was built in early 1700.

So that rules out America the bricks can attest to that perhaps Britain or England. My guess somewhere in England. The writing is English. Another marking the number 20 is over the writing. The 20th bridge? Signifying the year 1720 approaching or 20 bridges to go to build? Perhaps computerized image could reveal some more about the bridge.

No Salt Diet

U P UNTIL I WAS HOSPITALIZED, I used a lot of salt. Since oxygen level went down I quit & salt that had not much to do with oxygen level high blood pressure. The oxygen level is different thing sent home from hospital now been 1½ wks. I have used up 6 travel tanks, it back on to ups to lows paint store bank. Been my goal to work undertaking these high blood pressure-still blood pressure kind of high but is lower if I watch salt intake there is salt in cabinet and a salt shaker (empty) on table my water intake more but not enough.

Today, I did some chores cleaned and threw away food older than 11 days.

Hard to do but in a couple times have I used salt on food, some with sugar I drink cold tea no sugar, even though I have diet sugar for Virus who visit somewhere. No salt. Cooked a sauerkraut mashed potatoes and Polish sausage, maybe a pinch of salt in sausage?

My blood pressure has gotten lower still a little high.

Since I know longer use salt blood pleasure has gotten lower around 140/82 oxygen levels fluctuates 89-80 need to get it up to 91 or 92 still no quite use to no sugar in tea, have not used it in coffee for a long time.

Guess I just go on a fruit diet except for apples & salt them but if no salt still can eat a apple.

Guess salt part is out, food was given out. I got navy beans have back bacon & ham I can put in them. Set them out to soak in water over night. Found some ham in frig; threw it into a pot of beans soaking overnight in morning I will begin cooking them. Should be ready for supper meal, don't have any corn bread can't add any salt. Between you and me I can't add any beano.

I do have a can of navy beans I'd add them, might be what I need, to give them that navy bean taste not in any military. The only one eating them will be me and Mrs Smith if she don't like; I'll eat them all myself. Can't wait for this evening. My pot of navy beans will be done.

If I got my $3400 in bank today-66.75 insurance maybe buy more glue and pick up some stir sticks from Williams paint store.

Time for my walk to Health Food Store, I bought a timer to cook with. Think I will take it with me to maybe while at the V.A, and the second-Tuesday-I might see if my primary care doctor at V.A.-check cholesterol levels? It's getting to be a problem finding out how health people want to be in good health. I'm 72 now can't do things I did when I was young.

Maybe the no salt diet, even though salt shaker remains on kitchen table, so doe's diet sugar pocket to buy them for a neighbor; she has sugar diabetes. Today I'm salt and sugar free, but a new problem has arose, low oxygen level. That has me traveling with oxygen tank. Hate it.

Just when I think I'm getting better a new problem with my health arises, if I keep an eye on oxygen where the oxygen is line as much as I can it will go away? As far as my nurse goes have to wait till Tuesday, 5 days to see if she is still with me, if not I'll need to get new nurse to help me.

Robert's Struggles with Oxygen Tanks

RECENTLY DISCHARGED FROM MIAMI VALLEY North. Through premier health, I returned to my apartment with oxygen tanks & travel tanks-one home converter to oxygen and an emergency tank. Directions for use. A 24 hour use of the tanks is 1, a deep hate of them is a good reason for wearing them, hope of oxygen levels get back to normal a stay there. Struggles with keeping oxygen tubes staying in nose (keeps coming out.) Don't notice for 1 hour when noticed not on puts them back. Oxygen level will not return if not used at least 20 hours or more tubes coming out especially while sleeping. Maybe if he takes them to face while sleeping they will stay in nose? Robert thoughts are even with oxygen going in nose he sleeps breathing through mouth therefore some oxygen escapes out through mouth.

It has been a week since leaving hospital 15 hours of travel oxygen used since departure from hospital. Hard to tell how much he was used from Home Unit. But the less he uses it the less it helps. He works on keeping the oxygen going. And keeping mouth shut; so none escapes airline. Keeping it attached to his nose is not the only problem tripping on the air line pulls it out of tank and Home Unit, why he has an emergency. He is reminded of when the electric went out if he needed oxygen then he still did not have emergency tank. How he is equipped with emergency tank if should the electric faults 2:19 AM cannot sleep. Cause believed to be oxygen air tub to nose keeps coming off Robert puts it back as soon as he notices it is not in nose, on 5th travel tank since leaving hospital. Later today or tomorrow 6th tried tank. This is getting to be too much, going to bed will finish latter today.

Air lines to nose keeps coming off if busy does not notice off. As soon as Robert notices he reattaches to nose.

Today Thursday June 27 I'm setting at desk with oxygen on, was setting at desk I made opposite bath room making a few repairs to picture frames found card to game system play station 3. Cord from play station in TV broken was supposed to introduce to my home nurse. I over slept I guess. She never showed.

This oxygen getting to be a pain trying to stay home because I do not want anyone seeing me wearing it.

Past 9:00 already took meds time now 10.58 pm 10 hundred hours.

Air hose trips me up.

Setting at desk looking at a picture of O Neal played for Florida basketball later played for Cleveland owns couple business, and advertises a heat pain relief. He is in a brown suit black tie white shirt his hand is adjusting tie, air hose trips on it can't keep it on. Getting a little use to it my goal get rid of it, for now put it on and leave it on, is best thing to do. I have no money today tomorrow $134.00 even if insurance collects $134.00-66.40=$67.98 in bank tomorrow.

The river that passes my back window

The River

THE RIVER THAT PASSES MY back yard is not a river at all. It's not even stream or creak. Not even a puddle. Across the back of my apartments is a field beyond my back yard. As far as I can see across the field is green birch or oak maybe suppress. I don't know I have never traveled in direction what I'm told is it is the river called still water. Recently I was in Miami Valley North looking out my window I saw no river there either but a therapist told me. Stillwater River was near there. Englewood-a place I remember going fishing when I was a kid I would spend all day at the damn.

I had no idea that Trotwood and Englewood were neighbors. When I was young Englewood was 40 miles or more away. Maybe 60 miles. Now it seems they are right next to each other. Also Vandalia and Fairborn a long way. My priest comes from Fairborn and the man who takes up collection plate is from Vandalia. People leave here travel west thinking they will get to Dayton I guess if they take couple turns and head east the will get to Dayton. If I leave my apartment catch bus East Dayton bound I am West Lewisburg, Eaton Indy then Richmond Indy. Also when I was young people said south was Columbus.

As an adult I know Columbus is north of Dayton closer to Cleveland I really have no idea what is south maybe where I meet my wife Clermont County Batavia Waynesville area not been there since marriage to wife lived there about 6 or 7 years 1975-1976 72 78 maybe?

According to a newspaper I live in what is called 5 rivers still water, little Miami big Miami possibly I would say Ohio River somewhere in Miami Valley but Columbus mostly I think Butter township again north still have no idea what rivers or river is south. Or should I say the nearest river beyond the field and green trees is still water River the closest I've been to Stillwater River is Englewood Miami Valley North Hospital, a total maybe 4 days or week tops. I do hear the fishing is great at Stillwater River or Lake I believe it is. Might be a river. Someday I'll buy a fishing reel and rod on mosey, we'll have someone take me there and spend a day fishing hear there is a variety of fish at Stillwater. There is nothing else I can do except set around here writing short stories. When I have money I go east and visit people east of my apartment maybe I'll go south not much I know about what is south, as far as states go Texas, Florida, New Orleans, Georgia, South Carolina more north than south, South Carolina is actually north it is just the southern part of Carolina which is really the name of the state before dividing into north & south.

To tell you the truth they both North & South Carolina is south nothing north about going to either North or South Carolina both are south.

So in the conclusion of this story, it would be good advice to know a little about Geography; or get a GPS.

Red Dot Arizona

RED DOT ARIZONA IS ONE of the hottest towns in Arizona. Temperatures has been up in the 100's on a cool day maybe 81° or 85°.

Raymond Spade owns a small farm too hot for anything bigger. By the time veggies were picked most would be searched from the blazing heat.

Raymond is looking into installing 12 sprinkler systems. They are needed to keep the fruits and vegetables watered also he is installing other sprinklers all around the property. Keeping the whole property moist is a good thing. The next year's crop might be rotated maybe a lot of water needed for the new crops maybe not. Just to be sure Raymond crops planted this year is corn; wheat; cauliflower; beets; fruits planted were peaches; apples; grapes and strawberries.

Next year it will be different. The strawberries will become raspberries, the apples in the Apple Orchard will be red delicious instead of winsome.

Raymond has already changed over all except for the grapes he has on the southern part of his property. He has not decided whether to plant red; white, green or purple grapes looking at his record look he sees that in the past this area he had planted, red grapes and white, he would change them to green grapes; and purple grapes.

This year he's in studying climate for the year. That way he can figure out which grapes grew best and what month he must plant his seed. His survey showed what grapes grew in the area. He is going to go with red and white grapes. He also sees where Roman and Italian lettuce grows best, to make the changes, he has already bought the seeds and he knows where they will most like. He had planned. He began to plant the watermelon & the honey dew.

This was good year for Idaho potatoes and green beans; a good combination.

It is also good to grow peas and white beans.

Raymond had purchased a lot of seed, he bought barrels worth; some were mixed with other seeds, Raymond did not have the time to sort through the seeds he had already bought. He hired 4 men to sort out the seeds each barrel had four different kinds of seeds.

With 4 empty barrels at each full barrel of empty seed the men began their sorting of the seeds. It took all the morning hours to sort out 16 barrels of mixed seeds. The men had finished sorting. Raymond payed them each $50.00 $200.00 total for all 4 men.

Raymond put all 16 full barrels of kind on the back of his truck. He set them in the top of the rows again he hired men to plant the seed, because it was a long process each received $100.00 at dusk; the end of each day. Once planted all there was left, to water them with the new sprinkle system he had installed there was a main water control at the fork of the river noon time Raymond switch the water valve to get water to the seed that had turned to plants. Raymond turned the valve water ceased to flow eastward and went down stream to the sprinkler systems or the western area of the property. He would plant corn-sweat hard and Indian corn, only at the end of the year at picking time would he be able to which was more profitable.

Jake & the Bull Dog

JAKE WAS WALKING PAST A pet shop. Looking in the window he saw 4 puppies 3 were white puddles, the fourth was a brown boxer.

Jimmy took a liking to the brown Bulldog setting at the back of the window. It looked so lonely. Jake wanted to be the brown Bulldogs friend.

Jake opened the entrance door to the shop. Standing at a counter was the Pet Shop clerk. "Hello." The clerk said. "Hi" replied Jake. "Can I help you?" Clerk asked. "Can I see the dog at the back of the display?" "Sure." The clerk went to the back and picked up the pup.

"Here." The clerk said as he handed the pup to Jimmy, Jimmy took the pup in his arms. As soon as it was laying in his arms; Jimmy was petting the Bulldog pup. "Has he got a name?" "No" petted the pup. Starting from its head down its back then to the tip of its thin tail. Over and over he stroked the Bulldog pup. "How much you want for him?" $35.00 the clerk said. Jake reached in his pockets. In the right was $15.25. Jimmy reached in the left pocket $18.00-in total had $34.25. Jimmy was $100 short. The clerk would not sell the Bulldog pup for less than $35.00. Jake ask the clerk if he would not sell the pup, he offered the $34.25 to the clerk to hold until he returned with o the $1.00. The clerk replied "I cannot take your money without giving you the pup. "I cannot give you the pup for less than $35.00."

Jake put his money back in his pockets all in the right pocket. Quickly Jake ran out the pet stores door as fast as he could he ran home.

Up the stairs to his room. Pulling out the top dresser draw Jake pulled everything out. No money except for one lonely quarter. He needed 75 more cents. Jake pulled out the second drawer he found no money. Jake searched the remaining 2 drawers. He found no money. On his bed room floor was 2 pair of pants. He searched the pockets he found 25 cents only 50 cents more, Jake ran down stairs and searched under the coach cushions. He found no money. Jake went to the kitchen. He searched all cabinets and utensil draws no money.

Jimmy looked at the clock above the kitchen sink. 15 mins to 5:00. Jake's father came home from work. "Dad" Jake said I desperately need 50 cents. Mr. Thomas reached in his pocket "I have no change at all." Let me see if I have $1.00 in my billfold?" "Yes I do." "Here son." "You can keep" the 50 cent change." Thank Dad.

Jake looked at the kitchen clock. 10 minutes till closing at the pet store. No sooner, than Mr. Thomas gave Jake the $1.00 was he out the door and running one block, two blocks and a half. Jake was breathing hard as he reached the door of the pet store. Jake had made it 1 minute before closing.

I have the $35.00 for the Bulldog pup. He handed $34.25 to the clerk your 75 cents short. Jake reached in his left pocket no money. He then reached into his right pocket 75 cents.

The clerk filled out the pups papers. "The name you are/giving him?" "Oh!" I have not thought of one. I need one for his papers. I'll name him after myself. What is your name the clerk asked. "Jake." "Jake-what?" "Jake Thomas." The dog's papers were signed naming the pup Jake Thomas. The clerk explained to Jake a dogs papers are like your birth certificate and the dog takes your last name and whatever you name him his first name.

The clerk handed Jake the dog and its papers. "Thank you" Jake and his bulldog pup Jake Junior was out the door and at Jake's home. Right away Jake made a bed for the Bulldog pup. Then Jake made a food and water bowl. Jake set Jake the Bulldog down on the floor from that day on Jake had a Bulldog on his heels then became best friends Jake did not go anywhere.

Jake the Bulldog grew and after a year was a full grown brown Bulldog.

Mr. Long Sleeve

Mr. Daniel Keaton a long time resident of Mercer County; owns his own Metal Company. Mr. Keaton got into the metal business when he was 20 years of age, before he started his business he went to Mercer County Trade School. While at the Trade School he chose Metal Working as his intended Trade. He attended the Trade School 4 years then took a break then entered as a beginner; those were the rules. The Trade School was 64 year work training in a specific field. Mr. Daniels chose Metal Working Shop. It has been 2 months since finishing the Trade School. The rules cannot re-enter for 1 month. Mr. Daniels had left the Trade School 3 month, Mr. Daniels entered Trade School Metal worker advanced. That meant he has experience working with metals.

As before Mr. Daniels was given a student number that identified him as being enrolled in program. Mr. Daniels first assignment, demonstrate metal working skill or skills you have. Time limit ½ hr. For the next ½ hour Mr. Daniels demonstrated foraging, bending & shaping skills. Connecting with sedaline torch and lead.

Mr. Daniels had more metal skills but ½ hour was not long enough to demonstrate them.

The skills he did show was enough to get him enrolled back into the Trade School for another 4 years. While taking the Trade School course Mr. Daniels pulled luck his arm to make it appear normal. Same size as his left arm. Measuring his arms Daniels found both arms to be the same length.

On his shirt the left was smaller than the right sleeve when he wore that particular shirt everyone called him Mr. Long Sleeve. He thought it was pretty catchy and added a foot to the right sleeve. It was not long until no one. Mr. Daniels was in his fourth session second year when his shirt sleeve was welded accidentally to a project Mr. Daniel was working on. In a frantic move he pulled, jerked, and tugged. When he had finished the shirt sleeve remained attached while pulling and tugging and jerking in the shirt sleeve it stretched out. Also his arm had stretched the right one.

It appeared his right arm had stretched a bit. It appeared it was longer than the left. For 6 months Mr. Daniels was called Mr. Long Sleeve. After the 6 months Mr. Daniels was never called Mr. Daniels again. Whenever someone saw him they called him Mr. Long Sleeve.

It came to pass that whenever he signed his name he signed it Mr. Long Sleeve. He still had it in his birth name. But since everyone in town was calling him Mr. Long Sleeve; they accepted his signature as his nick. It has been a couple years since he was called Mr. Long Sleeve, that when he heard someone call him Mr. Daniels he ignored them and went on his way. When someone addressed him as Mr. Long Sleeve. He turned and "Yes" in the deep voice he had. He never answered to Mr. Daniels again.

One day when Mr. Daniels (Long Sleeve) was working in the eastern side of the property Mr. Sims his neighbor called him Mr. Daniels. Mr. Long Sleeve new not whom Mr. Sims was addressing? Mr. Sims called out his name again. Why was Mr. Sims looking at him when he was calling someone else? Mr. Sims; Long Sleeve asked "Why are you looking at me when you call someone else's name out? I am calling out to you; Mr. Long Sleeve. I am not Mr. Long Sleeve Mr. Daniels said. "Yes you are." "Do you not remember when working in the metal workshops you shirt sleeve caught up in a metal cutting machine?" "It stretched out your right arm sleeve; from then on everyone began calling you Mr. Long Sleeve." "Mr. Long Sleeve" is your nick name.

My memory is a jar these days. I cannot say I remember being called Mr. Long Sleeve. Could you address me as Mr. Daniels? "I suppose so." Answered Mr. Sims.

It did not take long for everyone to call him by his birth name. Mr. Daniels was never again called Mr. Long Sleeve.

My Pillow from Cleveland

6 YEARS AGO I WAS SETTING hear looking out my window. In my apartment; probably writing another ten page story. 6 years ago I was setting at the same window peering out it into the cornfield, Wheatfield, open fields. The farmer who plants it rotates his crops yearly. This year it is corn. Maybe field corn sweat corn or sweet corn?

That few years ago, I wrote a 10-story book called Robert's Short Stories for families. The difference this year is I'm writing looking out the same window. It is early in the morning; but pitch black out and quiet as an empty room, a pair of green curtains; unwashed about a half year hangs in the window, in a non-moving way. The place I wrote in 6 year ago-was a cheap and table.

The Shy Fox

THE RAIN FLOODED THE FOREST, outcome leaves floated down stream thrown away candy bar raps and sugar bags floated down stream also from people who lived on the river.

A soon to be mother fox looked for refuge on the banks of the river.

After half hour of searching the grey and rustic female fox found a dry spot inside a burrowed-sully. She laid her head down on a pile of leaves the winds had blown in.

Expired from being in the heavy rains and her unborn baby, the grey-rustic fox wasted no time falling to sleep.

The unborn became rushless from the cold of her mother's pouch. Often changing position several times the unborn had made its way to the delivery chamber. There was no turning back. The unborn was about to be the born.

The unborn fox saw light and followed the birth chambers into the light. The next four steps lead the unborn out of the birth channel and onto the forest floor.

The grey & rustic fox knew she had given birth she could move freely, she looked around 2 feet in front of her lay a light grey and light brown infant fox. The now mother fox knew what she was seeing was her unborn now born baby.

Mrs Grey fox swept up her baby and took it to a nest she had made for it. Paying it gently on a bed of soft leaves. Then herself. Together they both slept the remaining 3 hours of the evening's night.

When they awake the rustic mother new she had to teach her child fox the ways of the fox. She knew she had to teach him how to hunt for food and how to mingle with other foxes.

The new born kept a small distance from the mother and when mother was in the baby sight it ran away or found something to hide behind. Mother Fox knew something was wrong she had seen of foxes with their young and they stayed close and when others were around they did not run away.

Miss Grey and Rustic Fox kept a closer eye on her young baby watching its reactions to others, not just foxes either.

She had seen this reaction in a friend of hers; baby girl fox her friend told her it was from being shy.

Miss Grey and Rustic Brown Fox saw that it was true her son was a shy fox. She asked her friend what to do? Her friend said make him not shy away, when she sees him shying away force him to stay or approach what he is shying away from.

Mother Fox did just that and her son quite being so shy. But not all the way shy.

She kind of liked that a little shyness but not enough to affect your life.

Miss Grey Fox has not named her baby. He is 3 weeks old and just as big 3" inches tall. 3 inches long he is growing rapidly. Miss Grey Fox has thought of several names. Tiny because he is smaller than most foxes his age. Edward Fox after his father or a dozen other names. Oneel after a baseball player. After going down a list of names she got from a name book, she still has not picked out a name. *My young fox what can I name you.* A name slips my tongue. The small young fox still not trusting and a little timid hid behind a tree when others came around. The little fox was not a competitive little creature nor was he friendly to another. He was not violent either.

The young fox was not happy about his size all the others were larger and seemed to get along.

The timid shy fox was even shy around his mother after 4 weeks the shy fox still had no name. Miss Grey-Rustic Fox had come down to two names because he was so shy-he thought of the name Shy because he was so little she thought Little Fox. And because he was timid she thought of Timmy.

What kind of name was little, or even shy. Shy sounds like a girl's name she did not want others making fun because his name sounded girlish.

Only one name Timmy. But timid was no name either, so she dropped the d and named him Timmi which became Tim.

Tim got use to his name he liked it very well. Once Tim got use to his name his shyness & timidness went away and Tim was no longer a shy and timid fox.

Simond Stadler

SIMOND WAS WORKING IN HIS back yard when he heard a loud noise; coming from the forest. It was the cracking of trees falling. Brutice Lumber Company was cutting down trees. They were clearing out land for a new housing development. It was called Clear Water Housing Projects. It would be a middle class neighborhood. Rent for a single bedroom; bath, laundry room and kitchen $298.50.

Mr. Welch the owner of the Construction Co. struck a deal with the property owner. He would clear the land, level it for the new housing projects, to begin building a community. That would be Clear Water. Homes for the elderly.

Simond went on about his work. He was varnishing some new furniture his brother in-law had made. Jake Conners was a furniture maker the furniture Simond was varnishing was wooden bunk beds not a double but stacked Simond had already put on one coat. It had dried and he was halfway varnishing the second time. When he heard the cracking of trees falling to the ground.

Simond was sorry to see the trees behind his home fall but who was he to get in the way of progress?

Simond finished the second coat of varnish. He would let it dry then apply the third. Three coats of varnish would weatherize the tables and chairs he was working on was going to be patio furniture. Simond had made a deal to build and weatherize patio furniture for all the apartments at the apartments. They would be 500 apartments in 43 story apartment buildings. Simond had only done 20 patio table and chairs. It looked as if the varnishing would take 2 or three years.

Simond had just about finished the patio furniture for the first of 5 buildings. He had been working on it 8 months. Simond dipped his rag in a bowl of varnish. He spread the varnish over the last of a 4 chair one round table spreading it as evenly as he could. One last stroke; then onto the next patio.

As Simond made his last stroke he could hear more trees falling.

To Simond in a way that was another apartment building being built; and that meant more patio furniture.

The apartments were finished but Simons' agreement was to make patio furniture even after original furniture had worn out.

Simond was never hurtling for work sometimes he had to make time for a break just to let the varnish dry.

Simond set the table and chairs he had been working on a side. He began work on another. It seemed as though the patio furniture never kept coming. One set after the other.

Simond also made repairs to patio furniture he had once made. A small repair fee of cost & $6.00 labor charge a flat rate not $6.00 a hour.

Simond looked at the clock over the kitchen sink it was 6:00 pm.

Simond hung out the rag she had used. They were good for at least 3 more varnishings.

Simond was given a shop where he kept his varnishing equipment, he put the lid back on the varnishing bucket check his time out. Then headed home.

When Simond got home he made a vase of raspberry tea. Simond himself had bought a set of patio furniture. While sipping his tea Simond looked before him; and admired the work he himself had done.

Printed in the United States
by Baker & Taylor Publisher Services